CW00520119

SUSANNA HARUTYUNYAN

RAVENS BEFORE NOAH

A NOVEL

PUBLISHED WITH THE SUPPORT
OF THE MINISTRY OF CULTURE OF THE REPUBLIC OF ARMENIA UNDER
THE "ARMENIAN LITERATURE IN TRANSLATION" PROGRAM

RAVENS BEFORE NOAH

A NOVEL

by Susanna Harutyunyan

This book was published with the support
of the Ministry of Culture of the Republic of Armenia under
the "Armenian Literature in Translation" Program

Translated from the Armenian by Nazareth Seferian

Proofread by Emma Lockley

Author photograph on the back cover by Dirk Skiba

Book cover and layout interior created by Max Mendor
Publishers Maxim Hodak & Max Mendor

Ագռավները Նոյից առաջ (Ravens before Noah)
by Susanna Harutyunyan

© Սուսաննա Հարությունյան
Agreement by ARI Literary and Talent Agency

© 2019, Glagoslav Publications

www.glagoslav.com

ISBN: 978-1-912894-57-4

A catalogue record for this book is available from the British Library.

SUSANNA HARUTYUNYAN

RAVENS BEFORE NOAH

A NOVEL

Translated from the Armenian by Nazareth Seferian

GLAGOSLAV PUBLICATIONS

She had promised to kill the child as soon as it was born. Her payment for assisting the woman's childbirth was supposed to be thirty eggs—half of them turkey eggs—although her midwifery usually ended up providing her with ten hen eggs and all the curses directed at the child when he or she misbehaved ("Damn the midwife that brought you into this world..." they would shout, convinced that the person who first touched the newborn also passed on her character traits to the baby). Killing a newborn was more expensive—in her case—she received the green shawl the day the women gathered at the Spring saw Nakhshun double over, fall to her knees and groan in pain. Two of the women took her by the arms and dragged her home, while Bavakan, the mason's wife, glanced at a few women, including Sato, indicating that they should follow her.

Whenever the labor pains subsided, Sato would step outside.

"Well?" the women who were gathered at the door would say, spearing through the silence with their expectant eyes and rubbing their frozen hands together.

"Not yet," Sato would counter, spinning on her heels and stepping back inside, taking a sip of apple vodka, kicking some wood chips into the furnace and, squinting her eyes at the sensation produced by the smoke, she would shout to those standing at the door, "Open the skylight."

"The moonlight will fall on the mother," they would respond from outside.

Then Sato, coughing from the smoke and wiping her watery eyes, would approach the woman in labor. "The baby is coming feet first," she would explain to the woman, weakened in her torment, "Let's wait a little more. If it doesn't turn around, I'll reach in and help it." She would tap the blanket on the woman's legs, caress her forehead and sigh as she looked into her eyes. "This is our pain as women, and we have to bear it. Who can we complain to?" The strong vodka, which they had given her to disinfect her hands, had already dropped to half the original level as she came and went. She recalled the green shawl she had picked up and thought to herself that the women would kill her if she did not remain true to her word. Harout had first brought the shawl a few months ago at the request of the cobbler's wife, who had wanted to put it on the traditional tray of gifts and take it to her future daughter-in-law's house. But, feeling sorry for the woman in labor, the cobbler's wife had agreed to give it up during the conversation itself, when the women of the village had just started to convince Sato, and the tailor had completed it in just half a day so that Sato would not go back on her word. Later in her life, past the age of ninety when she had lost her family and her memory, Sato's disintegrating consciousness would only recall the green shawl from this whole experience, and she would then search the whole village for it, "My shawl… who took it, who did you give it to?"

They would reply, "Look in your chest of clothes… or in the folds of your bedding…"

"Oh, you naïve Armenians," Sato would exclaim as she kept looking high and low for her shawl, "It's gone… my shawl has flown away, it's on the road to Erivan… in Harout's carriage… They stole it, what will I do now?" But back then, in the warm aroma and whispers of Zaven's bakery, the women had suggested that the baby had to be freed through the woman's belly. She agreed with them.

"How strong can a newborn be? All you need to suffocate it is to just press hard on its nose and mouth."

But when she saw that the child was not coming into this world alone—the woman was giving birth to twins—she realized that this was not something she could do. Had it been one baby, it would have been fine. She would have told the woman that it had been stillborn; so many lives had been snuffed out by those hands… she decided who lived and who died. How many times… She had assisted that motherless girl recently, the immature daughter of the blacksmith. She had kept her at her house for a week and filled buckets with dung, telling her to carry them and empty the fresh droppings on the dung heap so that the heavy labor would cause a miscarriage. "Why have a baby who would keep reminding you of your humiliation?" she tried to persuade the girl. But the buckets were probably not heavy enough. Whatever she gave her to eat or drink, it did not make a difference… Then they put a millstone on her belly for two days. Her back cracked and her dorsal muscles strained, but the fetus did not detach from the womb. Then a stream of clouded and bloody fluid came out and the miscarriage occurred. The fetus was seven months old, like this one... it was healthy, a boy... It fell on the rug and started to cry, but she did not approach it to cut the umbilical cord. It screamed for two hours, its voice rang out in the world, but it did not die. She had fled from the room and taken refuge in the barn, leaving the mother and her aborted child to face each other... If only the weather had been better, Harout would have helped her find a childless family somewhere—Erivan, Bayazet, Aran—and they would have given them the baby. But it was a winter like this one—even colder—and the baby had been a healthy one, its umbilical cord uncut, and it screamed so much... It suffocated in its own screams. It had been easy on that occasion, she had not had any fears or doubts. Everybody knew that that immature girl could not raise a child and her father had been an old and lonely man... There was no other way. The blacksmith had even promised an extra sack of flour. But it was different with this woman in labor. She had twins, and such were their cries and moans while yet unborn, that even those on the other side of the door knew that they were healthy babies. All but Harout—had he known, he would have clubbed their heads off then and there, and cast them aside... Or the ultimate punishment would be meted out—the horse that Harout would groom and keep for special cases. She had seen it once, early in the morning, she did not even know what that poor slave had done wrong... But she saw Harout kick the horse hard in the balls, and the animal set off wildly, dragging the man behind it, ripping him apart against the rocks... who better to judge him than the rocks? And when someone asked him, "What happened to that man who was carrying the salt rock last week?"

Harout replied half-heartedly, "He didn't fit in... he left." Who could dare ask Harout another question or demand an explanation?

Those thoughts about Harout caused Sato to break out in a sweat, alternating between hot and cold. She felt her neck grow wet and the blowing wind gave her goosebumps. Just like that night when Harout had been left out in the open sea and had inhaled the cold air into his lungs. His throat had ended up covered in pus and the sweat poured over him in waves... She had cleansed his throat with white spirit and given him an infusion to drink, and they had chatted away the time as they waited for his fever to subside. Harout had talked to her about the newcomers, "Sato, I have given you time to get them on their feet. Why haven't you done so?"

She had explained herself, "They are very frightened. The sun scares them and so does the darkness. They are afraid of the heat as well as the cold. People, the wind… everything scares them. They neither eat, nor drink; they don't communicate with anybody… Nothing that I know seems to have an effect on them… it's nasty, the way they've been frightened. Frightened isn't even the right word… they're deranged."

"If nothing you know is working, try something somebody else knows," Harout had groaned, his head burning hot with fever.

And the decision was made… The fear was there—the fear of the darkness, the cold, the fear of predators, but their fear of God did not bring them to their knees, for they were doing good deeds. And when the moon was swallowed and the world went dark, an evenly black ball like a raven's eye; Sato climbed on the Wild Horse and sped through the peace of the night. And the peace of that night was frightening—it consisted of groans, the screeches of hawks, the sighing of the wind drowning in the valleys, the crackling of the rocks pouring from the mountaintops… the peace of the night was a battle between the sounds of nature and cosmic silence— first one would rise up and strangle the other, then the latter would gather strength and crush the former… And Sato sped as she clung to the neck of the horse, unable to decide which side she should take. She had never been so afraid. She would have refused if it had been up to her. But the throbbing veins of the sweaty animal vibrated beneath her calves, and vapor rose along the sides of the horse from the heat they were generating, and she was afraid that if she did not fulfil the command, the horse with the trembling flanks would drag her from a rope made of its tail hairs and shatter her bones against the rocks, and nobody would bother to check when it was dusk whether it was her blood blackening on the stones or the sweat of the sun. She was the first person besides Harout who had left the village, and this was the first time in her life. She returned to the place where Harout had picked her up in the hills and secretly wrapped her in a carpet before carrying her away. She moved carefully in the dark towards the cemetery… Like a dog, she went down on all fours and dug around the first tombstone she could find, and pulled out the bones she could grab. She washed them in the night, then dried them, ground them lengthwise and roasted the bone powder in a *saj*,[1] mixing it with flour and producing dough. She then baked bread and distributed it to the migrants. The migrants ate it and, along with the bones mixed with flour, they digested their own fears.

Sato looked at the mountains in terror, where the fog that rolled in around their summits had strangled the clouds, and she trembled.

Along with the women who stood in expectation, Vardanush's son was wrapped in his mother's skirt, waiting for the newborn to cry, so that he could deliver the news to Harout. Harout had promised him a puppy, one whose ears had not yet been cut and who could be trained as a savage. The child clung to his mother's skirt and imagined how he would train the puppy to bark and paw at pieces of fat hanging before it. He stomped his feet as he heard the women complaining and unwittingly partook in Sato's panicked behavior, the unbearable cold of the night, and Nakhshun's suffering. "Some heir. Not even born yet, but he has already finished off the poor woman." The boy was surprised at his mother's words. The child had not yet come into this world, but everyone had been talking about him for such a long time, ever since the migrants had first appeared. Just like in death, when the person has long since gone away, but people continue to discuss their absent existence for ages.

The southern wind brought cold flakes, and the women's anxiety doubled. "Isn't it over yet? This is killing us!" "Perhaps she will die in childbirth." The boy felt sorry for Nakhshun. He had seen her dead once, and it had been a terribly sad and horrifying experience. He remembered the first day he had seen Nakhshun.

It was his sister's engagement party and he was once again playing the role of the herald. "When the guests arrive, know that they are like our instrument, the *zurna*. Whatever they see inside the house, they will trumpet it to the outside world." His mother had promised him some *halva* from the bride's tray of gifts and had sent him to the top of the hill so that he would let them know as soon as they brought the fish. But the carriage was running late...

A snake emerged from beneath the ground, from a corner of the tombstone. The snake was coming from the other world and had to emerge

---

[1]   A flat utensil used for cooking.

slowly, crawling, hissing and hissing, wrapping parts of itself over each other and on the ground. The boy waited for the snake to bring itself out, piece by piece, then jumped on a rock and watched in terror as the snake squeezed its ribs into the crack between the flat rock and the thorns, rubbing against him and hurting him as it slithered by. He waited until the reptile stretched and crawled towards the sacrificial table, which had grass and flowers wrapped around it. The sacrificial table was a heavy flat rock that had absorbed the sun and plenty of blood, and had been unable to bear its own weight, so it had slid off its earthen pedestal, and dragged itself lower… A thick cross had been etched on its side and that was where the neck of the sacrifice would be slit, blackened blood lay dry within the cross… the knives had been sharp and the blood had sprayed on to the grass, appearing like black and red spots on their blades, and their roots had absorbed the sanguine drink like a predator. The snake rubbed its slippery belly against the flat rock and strangled the cross beneath it, adding its own weight to that of the blood as it slipped off into the grass. The boy saw the freckled cloud in the thorns, right there between the stones beneath his feet, almost rubbing against his bare big toe. He bent down and carefully picked up the skin shed by the snake, and stuffed it into his shirt. He would take it and give it to his sister; she could braid it into her hair so that it would grow longer. He felt for the still warm lizard's tail in his pocket which, they say, attracted wealth, and sat on the bumpy rock, happy with the day's spoils.

They appeared. They were both young, healthy, with sinewy legs, accustomed to the whip… Alo had a *daghdghan*[2] on its head, sitting comfortably on its forehead, while Blo had a colorful bunch of hair on its right horn that actually consisted of carpet threads, its strings swinging in rhythm with the movements of the animal's head. The carriage driver whistled; the whistle snapped like a whip in the air. The oxen understood the command and moved forward, kicking dust. The cloud of dust did not rise immediately from beneath the feet of the animal, as it would with a speeding horse. It was slow, unhurried, just like wise men weighing their words before speaking. Stone and gravel rolled down the slope, knocking into each other in the cloud of dust. The boy, who was standing at the top of the hill, smiled

....

[2]   A piece of jewelry worn on the head or hung inside the house, supposedly to ward off evil.

when he saw the well-loaded carriage, the effort the oxen were making, and the carriage driver, who stood above them with the whistle hanging from his neck. When the wooden wheels savagely attacked the cracked surface of the flat rock on the ground and creaked past it, he raised a bell over his head, turned sharply towards the village and swung it as he ran towards the houses, shouting shrilly:

"The fish cart is coming… fresh fish! Fish!"

The oxen, exhaling vapor and snot, stopped in the village square. The boy smiled and caressed the sweaty, dusty head of one of the animals, then walked forward to unlatch the carriage. He pulled the sheet back and screamed… The villagers waiting for fish were petrified at what they saw, some shouting despite themselves, some covering the eyes of the children who accompanied them, some murmuring meaningless words.

"Sato!" Harout shouted, "Sato…"

"What?" Sato's indifferent voice was heard from behind someone's back.

"Make them talk tomorrow," he said, indicating the carriage.

"Son…" the old woman muttered, "I'm a midwife—I assist childbirths and abort babies…"

"You cure warts as well."

"Son…" the old woman muttered again and, arming herself with patience, began to explain to Harout that it was one thing to read a prayer and bury a grain of barley on the night of the new moon, but a resurrection was something else entirely… "The new moon is powerless in such cases."

"I don't care," Harout retorted. "They must talk to me in the morning. The rest is your problem… Let each family take one, and those who ate the butter and honey can take two."

"What would we do with these corpses?" Someone complained softly in the crowd, without having the bravery to step forward.

"We didn't steal that food," Vazgen's wife mumbled, "We found it and ate it."

Harout stared straight at her. The woman hung her head, silently approached the carriage and began to examine it.

"I'll take the pregnant woman. That makes for two people, like you said, right?"

"The pregnant woman already has someone. Simon is taking her."

"I… I…" old man Simon muttered in fear, "I can't take care of the child."

"Don't worry," Arusyak nudged him, "Corpses can't give birth."

"What about you?" Simon attacked, "Why have you let this happen to them? Whoever is guilty of it should bear the burden."

"He's right," the midwife Sato sniveled, "Who are these people?"

"Who knows?"

"Where were they? Where did you find them?"

"They came."

"Came? On their own two feet?"

"Yes, their own feet."

"Oh dear..." Sato grabbed her head, "We have been discovered."

Sato had that same look on her face now as that same day, but she was not holding her head. She bore her terror alone, she did not share it with anyone. She mumbled something—perhaps a prayer—and kept walking in and out, scattering dust on the threshold from her fist, and then rubbed her nose with surprise that this did not reduce the labor pains for the woman. The women outside kept raising and lowering their legs to keep warm, and consoled themselves by saying that only important people came amidst such suffering. And their awe towards the Unknown grew with these thoughts.

The midwife Sato took another sip of the apple vodka. When the twins were born around dawn, and the knife heated at the fire was washed with the apple vodka, she cut their umbilical cords as her hands trembled, she barely managed to escape through the back door... straight to the house across the street where Sedrak was dying; she was supposed to wash his corpse and prepare it for the burial. The women ran after her and asked, "Well?" "Hold on, will you, Sedrak is dying..." Sato evaded their questions. Vardanush put the boy's blue fingers into her mouth and warmed them with her breath. "Run home," she ordered, "Run, or you'll end up with tuberculosis. Harout will give you a puppy anyway. What else would he do with five female puppies?" And she watched the midwife from behind as she guessed, "It's a boy for sure... This one is leaving this world, that one is coming." And Sedrak's departure was just as laborious... The roosters had been crowing in his ears for more than a month. And he was asking for water from the Silent Spring every day. Everybody who had ever asked for that water had died soon after. It was a common last wish among the villagers, the final thing they desired in the world. But the Spring was stubborn... it made such a loud sound—coming from underground or somewhere—that people could not hear each other, but it produced no water. Nobody knew why the Spring bore that name. Had they dug it free in the past and lost it? Had it been discovered by chance? How had it come to be that that arid Spring had come to replace the angel of death? The ill and the elderly would spend moribund days and months until the Spring would decide that their time had come. It would burp, spurt out a few drops into the world, and those spending the night near the Spring would rush to collect the water so that they could bring it to the suffering, so that they would drink it and give up the ghost… What mattered was that the Spring existed, and stuttered to life as it spurted the water. It would burst through at some spots, showing itself to dispel any doubts and then disappear. They had to be smart, they had to hunt it down as one would hunt for an opportune moment. They had to quickly place their palms beneath the sprouting water and then rush the drink to the ill, even if it was just a sip. Everything concerning Sedrak took longer than necessary. The children of the village came and went for five days, but they could not bring any water. Then Harout went and came back with half a flask. Sedrak drank. "Aaah," he said, "That leaves only the roosters…" Sedrak meant something else when he said roosters.

"You should look for albatrosses," the villagers would joke, pointing at the winged creatures swaying above the waves, "What kind of a bird is a rooster if it can't even fly? It's just another animal…"

Sedrak would be surprised and say, "What a strange thing to say. If an albatross could feel the warmth of the sun the way a rooster would, what need would it feel to fly?" Whenever someone fell ill in the village, whether it was a happy occasion or a sad one, he would take some roosters and hang them from his hand with their legs tied and heads down, as he went to visit. When he walked, especially when he came across someone, he would look down triumphantly at the roosters who were tired of resisting and had simply raised their necks slightly so that their beaks would not strike against the ground. When he reached his destination, he would stay until the roosters had been killed and the table had been set… He would eat with his elbows on the table, chewing slowly and sucking hard, he would smack his lips and remove the chicken bones. The last time he had eaten a meal like that was when they had slaughtered the spotted rooster with the fair wattles. That had been Amo's last wish. That day, Sedrak had sat beneath a tree, put the plate between his knees and poured some homemade vodka. "May you go into the light, Amo," he said despite himself, out of sheer Christian goodwill, and he ate Amo's last desire. It was a good thing too that Amo had not managed to eat the chicken, he hadn't been ready in time. He would force his young daughter-in-law to bathe him.

"It is your duty," he would say, "To care for your father-in-law." He would strip down and enter the tub and when the daughter-in-law would bend over to pour water, he would let his hands roam freely. One day, as they led the flock of sheep out of the barns, the men of the district had caught him in the act and beat him up. "My younger son is impotent, his wife will end up leaving him. I'm doing this for the integrity of my family…" the womanizer Amo explained. He was a godless man, but when he was dying, his wife and sons were at his side, there was someone to hear his final sigh. He took a deep breath and, as the air crackled in his lungs, he asked, "Sato, you never saw my first wife, did you? How could you have, you hadn't arrived yet at the time. But it was you who bathed the second one…"

"She had a pretty body," Sato recalled.

"Oh, this is strange. Both of them have come after me, they are standing before me and waiting."

"Which one will you go with?"

"I don't know. I'll tell you once I go."

"How will you tell me if you've already gone?"

"If I have something to say, I'll find a way to say it, don't worry about that." A short while later, he moaned, "Sato, can you hear a rooster?"

"No," Sato replied, checking whether the water in the pot on the furnace was warm and whether there was enough to bathe a corpse.

Sato could smell the arrival of death, like hunting dogs could smell their prey. "His nose looks sharper," she looked over at Sedrak, whose eyes were closed, "There's not much time left." She decided to stay with him. She would wait, she didn't want poor Sedrak to be alone when the moment arrived. She thought that the village would pitch in to cover the costs of the funeral. She took out the kerchief that served as a wallet from between her tits, unfolded it, and arranged a few single notes in a row on the table, raising her fingers to her mouth each time to wet them with saliva, and separated the notes one by one. Then she regretted doing so, and put half the notes back. She looked again, and picked up one more. She glanced again at Sedrak, who was now barely breathing, with his eyes still closed. She picked up the last note as well and put it back in the kerchief, tied it up and stuffed it down her bosom. "All this work I'm doing is worth money, after all… Let the ones who are relaxing at home now chip in some money; they'll come tomorrow to a corpse that has been prepared without the slightest effort from them…" She got up and added half a bucket of water to the pot on the furnace.

The noise caused Sedrak to open his eyes. "Sato, do the village folk know that I'm dying?"

"I've mentioned it to them…"

"Well, then," Sedrak complained, "When are they going to return the roosters I had given them?" His eyes were directed at the door. Was someone going to walk in for a visit, with a pair of roosters hanging from their arm? And his eyes froze there, at the empty doorway.

Sato mumbled as she shut his eyes, straightened his arms and legs, pulled the cover over his face and rushed outside. "He's dead," she said to the gathered women, "The poor thing, go inside until I come back, so that he isn't left alone." She rushed to the woman in labor, wondering whom she should call to sit by the corpse at night… it couldn't be left alone, but she was so tired… there were so many cats in the village, they might come and deface the body…

And then the sun went down, without a coffin, like the gods… "The sun is lucky to have a place it can escape to," Harout thought as he paced in and out. The last time he was this anxious was back in his childhood when he was five—or seven—years old, and had bitten into a carrot only to find that his tooth had stayed stuck in it. They pulled out the other wriggly one by wrapping a thread around it and then tying the other end to a door, which Perch then kicked shut. The door slammed shut and took the thread and tooth with it, as well as Harout's childhood, hanging at the end. It was late autumn at the time, the same period as now, but no snow had come yet. He had sat there, shaking his clenched fist, rattling his fallen teeth in that palm, waiting for the moon to come out. The moon came quickly, rootless like a desert plant running before the wind. He sat on Perch's shoulders, looked to the sky, rattled the teeth in his fist again and shouted to the stars with all his might, "Take these wolf's teeth, give me a lamb's teeth." He used the same strength to throw the teeth through the autumn night towards the sky. Did the moon pick them up? What would the sky do with those milk teeth? He recalled that with a smile now. "Why a lamb's teeth? A lamb is innocent, yes, but it grows into a sheep." He would not ask for a lamb's teeth at this age, that's for sure...

The moon looked down with the cold stare of an insect trapped in resin. The moan spread, coming from an unknown source. The sounds of howling at the moon stretched out, bringing all kinds of thoughts to Harout's sleepless mind, breaking down his soul and uncovering his crusted wounds. The pain rose within him, hurting at his very roots, and reached his throat, strangling him. "I wonder what's making it sing like that, moaning so bitterly... no prey to be found? Do his nostrils hurt from a lack of the smell of blood? Oh, brother wolf..." he sighed, "If my pain were yours, you wouldn't even be able to make a sound." On other days, dogs would be barking from a thousand spots. Each would encourage the other with its snarls, they would double down and drown out the wolf's lone howling. But today it was as if all of the dogs were dead, as if the wolf had entered an unprotected village and was tearing people apart left and right as it howled at the moon. "What a sweet sound it makes," he was awed, "Such long howls, so heartfelt... like a prayer." And then he felt terrified by his own thoughts and pleaded, "Oh God, please help me so that my prayer never turns into a howl."

One of the shortcomings of life is that blood cannot be castrated. And the memory of that blood was coming now, thump, thump, thump... With the rhythm of a woodpecker, observing regular pauses, it was knocking stubbornly and dully. Each breath he took felt like a nail being driven through his heart. One of his parents had probably been murdered by a knife through the chest, and that pain had transformed into a sanguine memory. He hadn't even seen a parent in his dreams, because he did not have an image of either of them in his memory which he could resurrect in his sleep. Of course, he could fill the void in his memory using icons and imaginations, but that would be fake, and his intention was not to deceive himself.

He had never managed to ask Perch whether they had come on horseback or on foot. He hadn't even asked how they were related. He had said that he was his paternal uncle, and that was that. Otherwise, he wouldn't have heard the rumbling coming from the grain silo amidst the wailing and crying on the day of the massacre. He wouldn't have pulled off the shawl from his mother lying flat on her face, he wouldn't have quickly collected the soil inside the crib, which mother placed there to quickly absorb the baby's urine and keep the bedding dry. He wouldn't have wrapped Harout in the cloth and fled, knocking his foot by accident against his father's head, which had rolled into the yard after being chopped off, ending up near the chickens' feeding bowl.

Perch knew everything. There were more faces in his memory than were even in the Bible. Each of them was carefully arranged in a frame and nailed to the wall of his memory. It's too bad that he aged quickly and the autumn migration flights from his memory started early. In a single night, all the faces and incidents flew off flock by flock, like the wrinkles disappearing from the face of the deceased—his mind was wiped clean and his blood lost its memory and he became a hollow reed. Perch cleansed his brain—as if intentionally—by directing that fountain of misery inward, in the same way that the waters of God's wrath washed over the world, but he left nothing behind. No memory, no Noah. His memory at first, then his sight, then his ability to speak… He cocooned himself in oblivion, like a male butterfly enclosing the love organ of a female so that nothing can enter or leave any more… He was free of everything that bothered him and could now live in peace. However, he would sometimes jump up in terror with no obvious cause, unconsciously looking left and right. The villagers took good care of Perch—they cared for him like they would the grave of a relative, or a family heirloom—perhaps a copy of the Bible with a silver cover that must be meticulously cleaned, kissed with awe, and wrapped in red felt, far from the eyes of strangers. That was probably the reason why he lived so long—so long that he dishonored both life and death, finding them both incapable, and humiliated them.

Yes, they lived long lives, as if forgetting to die, as if on purpose, as if the terror kept them alive… Life would abandon them, but the terror would not. It would crouch next to them like a loyal dog, licking their hands, rubbing against their feet, and even if it was the end, if the door was closed, it would still not go away. It would roam about, passing from lips to lips, like the secrets of ancient magic, relying only on trustworthy lips, not to be written, not to be documented, not to fall into hands with malicious intentions.

His heart began to beat anxiously when he thought of Perch—rapidly and with a kind of anger that can come only from injustice. He started pacing again. His leg hurt whenever he sat for a long time. It also hurt when he walked too much. And from the cold. But the heat hurt it more… If only his mother had dropped him more carefully in the wheat, if only she had held him from another part of his body... although that would have left him with a painful organ in any case, it was his destiny. If only his grandmother had been around. If she had been around, she would have strangled a chick right away and beat its body without plucking any of the feathers. She would have then placed the creature, still warm, on his hurting knee, and the bird—murdered but not yet completely dead—would have absorbed the pain into its own body.

"Are you asleep?" Sisak stuck his head into the doorway and then pulled his whole body through, groaning as he put a hand to his ribs, "Did I scare you? It's just me."

"Come in, I wasn't asleep, you didn't scare me..." Harout answered all his questions at once.

"Sato is finding it hard to manage. She's saying the child might die. Although, if that does happen, I guess it's for the best."

"How can death be for the best?" Harout was surprised.

"Anything's possible. I mean, would you call what they're living now a real life? Take this list..." he pressed a hand against his ribs again and groaned especially for Harout's ears, "This damn thing is killing me... my liver... my sister has come to see me, she's brought *halva*, but I can't have any. That bear has come down from the mountains and gotten into the graveyard, toppled a few gravestones. The stone of the hunter's dead boy too... His wife cried so much she went blind. But the culprit isn't a person, so you can't hope for revenge. What does that animal know about this world? But I've had a trench dug around the graveyard so we can put up a fence. All that remains is to set it up... So, what was I saying? Ah yes, take this list. The written word lives a long life, keep it somewhere safe because someone might need it after we're gone, you never know."

Harout picked took the list and looked at the sheet.

"Look at these last names—Keshishoghlyan, Gharagyozyan...[3] It's like they've managed to stay faithful both to themselves and the Turks..."

"That was the only way they could survive."

....

[3]   These last names, like some Armenian last names, consist of Turkish roots, e.g. Gharagyozyan comes from the Turkish for "the one with black eyes".

"Well, maybe they shouldn't have survived… what's so special about going to sleep and waking up, or drinking a cup of water, that could justify a sacrifice like this one?"

"It's easy to judge them… it's always easier to pass judgement on others," Sisak walked towards the door, still groaning and demonstratively pressing his hand to his side, "Good night."

He returned hours later.

"We need eggs, there are five missing… she's given birth, we need to pay Sato so she can leave. They haven't let me get any sleep tonight, I've been on my feet for so long… I said Nakhshun has given birth… it was hard—she nearly died… If only she had borne a son after all that."

"It's a girl?"

"Don't you wish it was just one girl?" Sisak sighed heavily, "Twins…" he flailed his index and middle fingers, hiding the other ones, "Twin girls. But there's one good thing—they're both very small. They might not make it."

Harout remembered how he had been sawing a log a few days ago and had called out to Harout junior for the sharpening stone. He had called and called… the boy was nowhere to be seen. He had been scared—could the boy have gotten lost in the valley? Then he calmed himself—the boy was with Varso, listening to one of her stories. Nevertheless, he went to look for him just to be sure.

The little hands were picking pebbles from the river through gaps in the fence. Each of them had found a pebble that was suitable for the game—flat, round, first the small one, then smaller, then smallest… The boys placed the river pebbles on top of each other and made a pyramid. Little Harout was standing some distance away, waiting for them to finish. He held a stick in his hand, ready to throw it and demolish the structure. He had shut one eye and was taking aim—he kept bringing the stick close to his face and then moving it away again. He would rush forward and jump, feigning a throw—his hand would leap forward, but his fingers would not let go of the stick.

Three boys squatted, arranging the stones on top of each other. The slippery river pebbles would slide off once a fourth or fifth one was placed on, and the structure would collapse on to the grass. The boys were grumbling with dissatisfaction as they restarted the arrangement.

"Get it over with," little Harout tried to rush them, "This is taking forever…"

"What can we do? It keeps collapsing," the little masons complained.

"Guys… come, quick…" Anush's six-year-old boy called them, trying to catch his breath, "She's out in the open… hurry! I'm on my way there now… Did you hear what I said? Out in the open! Let's go see! Come on, I'd rather die than lie about this, it's out…"

Little Harout ran after the small boy. The group of boys had just finished arranging the stones, but they forgot about the effort they had put into it and crushed the structure underfoot as they ran after them.

"If you're joking about this…" little Harout gasped, swinging the stick in the air and threatening the messenger.

"I swear…" the little boy grabbed the stitch in his side as he ran, "I saw her with my own eyes, you can see it out in the open, she was standing at the wall."

The boys hid behind the fence and were secretly watching Nakhshun. She was in the yard and had spread the bedding she had just stitched on the stone wall, extending it from end to end.

"Where is it?" one of the children whispered, looking at Nakhshun.

"Well," little Harout responded, without looking at his friend, his gaze steady at Nakhshun, "It's in her belly…"

One of the boys shouted without revealing himself from his place of concealment.

"Damned son of a Turk!"

"What the hell are you saying, you little whelps?" the senior Harout grabbed the boy who had shouted by the neck.

The smaller children retreated to the wall in fear.

"We weren't saying anything," little Harout mumbled, "We'd come to see a Turk."

"It was a difficult labor," Sisak explained, "Midwife Sato had probably taken a gulp or two when she washed up with vodka as usual, she slipped and fell on the threshold, her hard earned income from that night crashing against the floor in one second—thirty eggs, fifteen of which were turkey eggs…"

"I'll bring some more," Harout walked towards the corridor with the slow steps of a tired man, thinking about the newborns and sensing the draft blowing from the door that was loose at its hinges. He reprimanded himself mentally—on that cool summer night, when the fire was crackling in the *tonir* and the hot iron furnace sent pieces of ash flying, burning into the skirt of darkness… what business had it been of his? Why had he violated the tradition of not asking the newcomers any questions? Did he really need to know who they were? Would they live decent lives in the village? If they didn't, the horsehair rope and the wild horse were always an option.

Until that moment, he had never thought about it, he had never given proper thought to the day that the newcomers had appeared. That day had not boded well. He should not have dragged them over to the village. If he was cruel enough, he could have left them lying there in the sand, and in just a few hours, the wind that spat foam onto the beach would have killed them with the cold humidity it brought from the water…

The cool humidity of the cellar reminded him what a peaceful day it had been…

There were three of them on the lakeshore—the crow, the cat, and Harout. The wind, too. But the wind's legs were tied and it was rolling about miserably in the sand somewhere, exploding from time to time and casting sand on the waves, simply to remind them of its existence.

The crow perched on the branch like a statue, its neck sticking out as it stared unblinkingly at Harout's bloody hands. He was pressing his knife against a rock that was stuck in the sand and cleaning its blade with a bloodied rag. He would then stick the tip of the knife into the belly of a fish and slide it across its body, all the way up to the gills. He would cast the knife aside and grab the fish's innards in his hand, plucking them out deftly, and then throw them down at the cat while dropping the fish in a wooden jar buried in the sand. The cat—one eye green, the other yellow—sniffed the fish's guts with satisfaction yet again, purring at the pieces of fish entrails all around him. The crow would lose no time—it would drop and grab the guts, sliding them along the reddened sand as it lifted back up and flew far away. This did not bother the cat and it did not pursue the bird. It had exhausted itself by eating these corpses, and it purred with its eyes closed in the shade of a tree, its neck buried in its ample fur. Harout's right leg was tired of squatting. He would get to his feet, stand up and shake his leg in the air in an attempt to reanimate it. He would pick up the wooden spoon leaning against the reeds and walk up to the jar buried in the sand. He would stir its contents with the spoon and add fistfuls of salt on the fish, then stir again. He would drown the fish in blood and salt so that they would be well pickled, then he would return to his spot and squat again. A short while later, the crow would return and perch on the branch…

He used the sharp knife to roughly scratch out the scales and pour out his anger on the fish. "You're such an idiot…" Harout was arguing with Vazgen in his mind and once again dug his knife deep into the fish's abdomen—as if he was piercing an enemy's heart—and dragged it explosively up to its gills. He could not forgive himself; he should never have given it… he had come and started telling him a story of how, many years ago, in a previous life, he had met a Russian general near Bayazet, and they had chatted and laughed.

"Did you manage to laugh in Russian?" he had made fun of him.

"Ha-ha, you rascal, is there anyone else who can laugh like me?"

In the end, he had made a request—"My poor kids, they'd really enjoy it if I could play acrobat at home and amuse them…" And so Vazgen had stretched a tightrope and jumped up and down on it; he had stood down there and watched from below, clapping and happy like everyone else. And then the wind had come… "Was it the devil? Where had it come from on this sunny day?" The jester had his fake beard and mustache on when he rushed up, but he was clean-shaven when he came down. The wind had carried Vazgen off by the skin and taken everything—his clothes, the beard and mustache… bringing him down naked, like the day he was born. It lifted the beard and mustache that Perch had left and ripped it apart string by string, carrying it off into the sky.

The last thing that Perch had bought, the beard and mustache… Who knows where he had met those gypsies, in what language he had spoken to them, how much he had paid or what he had given them in return? The man had brought that fake beard and mustache and saw no problem in wearing it—Perch had used it first, then he had. He would put it in his carriage and go, roaming around the world. In Ararat, he would say that he was from Artashat, in Artashat he would claim to be from Erivan, in Erivan—from Bayazet, chatting away and seeing the world, selling his ware and trading items, always returning safe and sound to his mountains. Let them guess who he was if they could. But now they were going to be cut off from the world because of one idiot. "Damn it!" He hated Vazgen, but calmed himself.

"What's done is done... sooner or later, we will have to present ourselves with our real faces anyway."

He wiped his eyes with his arm. His heart always grew heavy when he thought of Perch. He had brought him up, taught him how to read and write, how to hunt... He could recall a thousand and one good things related to that man, but for some reason, thinking about him would always bring back the memory of that particular day. Perch was lying lifeless and cold, like a rock. When he held out a hand and shook him by the shoulder, he had never imagined that a human being could be so cold. He sent for Sato, who was massaging the aching bones of Bavakan's husband with bear tallow at that moment, even though she knew that it would not help him. She nevertheless held onto a vague hope that it would and when the patient groaned with pain, Sato would stop her massaging and ask, "Can you feel the relief setting in?"

"No, I can't," the patient was moaning through gritted teeth.

"In a minute..." Sato began to massage with greater fervor and slathered on some other oil as well, "It will help in a minute." Bavakan and her sister-in-law sat next to each other, their teary gazes watching Sato torture herself.

"If only he would die quickly," his wife was compassionate, "It would be a relief for him *and* for us."

"Don't rush God's work," the midwife hushed her, confessing deep within her soul that his death was the best option indeed, "You think you'll be better off once he's dead? Long-standing marriages are good because they bring stability to one's life. It's true that the life people share in such cases is often reduced to shreds—there is no love left and, in many cases, no respect. But when your companion dies, they take your life story with them. Your life ends up deserted, there is nothing left, nobody left to fill that space... And there is nothing left for you to do, but go after your companion. So you should be calling on God to give him life."

When she heard Perch's name, Sato got up immediately and shot out without covering the sick man's body, her hands still oily. By the time she arrived, Perch had quietly left—he had not said any last words, he had not looked at a particular person, he had simply gathered the life he lived and the one he had not, and gone. The only thing left of the once-glorious man was the handful of old bones huddling in the bed.

Without interrupting his scaling of the fish, Harout kept wiping his wet eyes with his sleeve, recalling with tenderness how he had picked him up and put him in the stone seat that Perch himself had brought over years ago, when he had noticed a passage under the Silent Spring. He had entered a city that was upside-down. He had taken out a churn, a gun, and they said that he had even found gold, along with that throne of stone. Naturally, he had brought that throne of stone on his second trip. And he had never dared go back in there, nobody else had the courage to go into that door either—not even Harout—because Perch had said there was no air to breathe there, only sulfur.

He would sit there until sunset, quiet and unmoving, looking neither upward nor down… His gaze uneven, he seemed to hold the world inside his eyes, and then he would shiver from time to time, like the Silent Spring. Harout watched him and thought that everything was directed at someone—a prayer, a curse, a blessing… Who was the person addressed by Perch's tearless sobs? Alas, there was no one. He had been tricked by both life and death. The villagers walked past and pretended nothing had happened, as if it was the same Perch, and they said hello from afar and talked to him.

"Good day, Percho, great news—my cow has given birth!"

"Hello, uncle… I just got married, we need to celebrate…"

"Oh, Percho *jan*, my mother has gone and left us the life she didn't live… Yes, we haven't marked the forty days after the death yet, but she was such a good person that I'm sure she has been crowned an angel without any Final Judgment."

Perch would remain seated there, still, and in the same position, like a breathing rock. But everyone that walked past would nevertheless consider it their duty to say something to him. People began to treat him in the same way they treated God—seeing him and saying a couple of words had become a necessity. They talked to him, asked his advice, shared their pain and worries, without expecting a response.

As soon as the sun went down, Harout would take him indoors. He would carry him and tuck him in bed, and it would be his turn to speak to him.

He recalled nothing of Perch's burial because he had been beside himself with grief… until the moment when the corpse moved near the entrance to the cemetery and sat up in the coffin, looking left and right in surprise. The people froze and dropped the coffin in terror, running away. He got up and stood there in the coffin, picking up the snow-white pillow from the ground. "Sato! Damn your father's soul! I had this pillow made for Harout's wedding. Why have you placed it under the head of a dead man?" And he walked home with the pillow under his arm. For three days, people were too scared to show up at their door or walk past their house. Perch had tasted death and this meant that he was no longer one of them, he caused terror. For three days, Harout would take him as usual and place him on the throne of stone, then carry him indoors in the evenings. On the fourth, he heard a noise at night.

In the morning, people saw with surprise that it was Harout sitting on the throne of stone. "Where's your father?" they asked.

"I was asleep, he opened the door at night and left," Harout sighed. For a few more days, people searched for Perch in the mountains and the valleys, but then Harout said that there was no point. "He did not like the death we served him, he has gone to search for the death he wanted…"

"We were seeing him off as we should—with tears, flowers, a memorial meal. If he didn't like it, that's his problem," the elders sighed in return, "May he go and die any way he pleases."

When Harout once again grabbed the innards of the next fish and pre-pared to throw it at the cat, he raised his head, his eyes dissolving in tears, and saw a group of ghosts in front of him. This was one of those places where it comes as a surprise to see another human being and Harout had grown mute as he looked at them with a shiver—so many people secretly existing in the mountains?

"Who are you, what do you want?" he called out, shocked, searching his mind for words or actions that are supposed to drive off evil.

"We…" an old man muttered, the words were picking themselves off his lips so slowly and painfully, it was like using tongs to pluck off fingernails. "We are not to blame… This is where the world ended. There is no way back, nor any path ahead."

As Harout had looked up and examined this disheveled, emaciated group, a young woman urinated right where she stood, like an animal. The wet sand flew this way and that, the cat mewed with displeasure. The crow pressed its wings close to its sides.

"An animal," Harout reached for the limestone and dragged his numb leg to get up, his eyes meeting the blank stare, like a blind person, of the woman's large eyes. "That is what death looks like," he thought with a shiver.

"We have no strength left," explained the old man, lost in his own beard and hair, "The poor thing does not even have the strength to squat."

Harout examined them in a state of panic. He knew that life always served up surprises and things always happened where you least expected them and when you least expected them. But why did that unexpected occurrence have to happen with him in particular? Suddenly, the newcomers flopped onto the sand one by one, like ripe fruit. "Only demons can be so weightless," Harout thought to himself. One of them tried to crawl, grabbed a whole fish and started to eat it. Harout stared in shock for a moment, unable to comprehend what was happening. "They're hungry," he realized and felt sorry, "They're human. Demons are not tormented by hunger—neither hunger affects them, nor their conscience, nor anything else… They are deprived of emotions." He ran towards the jar buried in the sand.

"That's not good, don't eat that," he said as he used the wooden spoon to dig out the pickled fish from the depths of the jar, which he then washed in the lake and brought to them.

"Take small bites."

Harout dragged them to the river that flowed rabidly from the mountains before turning into narrow streams until all that was left of its boundaries was the wet sand, the same way that animals mark their territory by urinating. He held them by their armpits and took them over one by one, throwing them on the wet green land of the river bank, then quickly splashed water on their faces.

"The village is close by," he said, "Gather some strength and let's go."

"There is no strength left," the old man moaned, "We'll stay here."

"You can't stay here, the night wind blows the skin off the beach at night and raises a sandstorm," he felt sorry he had not brought his oxen with him—they had foot-and-mouth disease and were locked in his barn, their hooves in grease and viscous snot covering their faces.

"Oh, we're dying, we're dying…" the old man whined, "After all we've seen, how much can our lives be worth?"

Some of them were managing to chew or lick the pieces of raw fish, while the others seemed to have gone lifeless with the fish in their hands and their hands helplessly lying in the sand. Small, red insects had gathered on the pickled fish and their hands.

Harout ran a bit further away and brought out a large net woven with willow branches. He cast it over the river like a dam right over the spot where its minor stream flowed into the lake. He first grabbed one handful of the net on his side of the river and used a stump to dig it into the soil, then jumped over the rivulet to the other bank and fastened the other end of the net in the ground with another stump. Then he jumped over the rocks jutting out of the stream and came back.

"Don't go too far… I'll send you some food using the river, everything you need… You can pick it up here… Until I come to get you," he showed them the dam he had formed with the net, now deep in the water, it had already caught some foam and weeds, and then he ran to the village.

Summer was gone in a blink in these parts… The stormy winds would pluck moss from the depths of the lake and bring it to the shore, clapping them onto the ground and bringing the aroma of water and algae. The waves would wash the algae onto the heated rocks of the beach and seem weaker as they retreated. Harout would usually lean on the rickety boats that had been lined up, upside down, their sides covered in tar, and watch the water for hours as the wind would blow sand on their hulls… When the waves exploded from the depths of the lake and hissed chaotically at the cliffs, they did not seem to know that they could not crack the rocks by ramming into them. What happened next would only be known to the white foam that remained from the waves after they struck.

Now the waves were advancing with a loud hiss, and they were bringing more of the same—foam.

Looking at the boundlessness of the lake, Harout asked himself, "Where did the flooding waters go? What did they take with them? What human sins were they asked to recompense? Are they under control? Did they retreat for another round? What other explanation could there be for what the newcomers were saying?" The waves broke upon the smooth stones with a crackle, pulverized when they touched their surface, and little trickles flowed back, running through the algae with the white roots that were dragged onto the sandy bottom by the waves before scratching their way out of the water and ending up in a knot on the beach rocks.

Harout breathed in the familiar slimy smell and tried to understand— who were these newcomers, what were they trying to say? With whom would he now have to share the boundlessness of the lake, the solitude of the mountains and their pain, as unexpected as a miracle? In November, the last time he had gone down to the world, he had not seen or heard of anything like that… He felt upset as he thought of how we would give his food to the newcomers, then get on this cart and, if there was any space remaining, he would bring some fish back with him. He would line up the pickled fish on the rocks and tell the children to turn them over from time to time. The sun would dry them and the wind would blow away the salt… He walked, wondering whether the food he sent over the river had been enough for them. At that very moment, Vazgen the *zurna* player was shivering as he ran to the river and washed up. He splashed in the water and washed his armpits, and closed off his right nostril with his thumb as he gathered air in his lungs and prepared to blow through the other nostril. But he had frozen after that. The water was bringing large pieces of cheese to him. He grabbed them and lined them up on the grass. The water also brought several mounds of butter, the traces of human fingers still frozen in some parts.

"Wow," Vazgen, dumbstruck by his good fortune, had taken out another whitish mound from the water and licked it, almost rubbing his nose into it. "It's honey!" As he licked it, his heart filled with suspicion, "Who would be stupid enough to throw these things into the river? It might be poisoned!" He fearfully examined a little jar he had just caught—it was full to the brim with buried cheese, flavored with oregano. Then another little jar—this one had *ghavurma*, the pieces of yellow fat still sticking to the meat here and there… He picked up a piece of cheese from the grass and bit into it. He froze for a second, concentrating on his stomach and the sounds it was making. "I don't know," he said to himself, "Let's wait a couple of hours. If I don't die, then none of this is poisoned."

When Harout returned, the immigrants were lying lifelessly on the blue sand, only the pregnant one was blinking her eyes open and shut.

"I sent some food over the river for you. Why didn't you pick it up?" he asked in surprise, looking left and right at the people on the ground.

"The river brought nothing," the woman barely managed to say through her dry, cracked lips.

He tore off a piece of the bread in this pocket, which he had put there to eat on the way, and stuffed it into her hand, but the woman was in no state to lift the bread to her mouth. Harout recalled how he would reduce bread to small pieces when he was a little child, and he now placed such crumbs into her mouth. But she was in no state to move her jaw either. He realized that he had to hurry. "I must use a cloth to drip water into her mouth." He stopped his cart near the bushes, on the wet sand, not too far from the river. He placed the migrants on it and returned to the village. Throughout the journey, he tried to talk to the woman, but the wind made any conversation impossible—any spoken words were meticulously shredded and ripped apart, leaving only fragments of sound to mix with the blowing sand.

When he arrived, the villagers were expecting fish.

In the cold air of the cellar, he ran a hand beneath the basket to feel for turkey eggs. He placed several of them in his pocket and held the remaining ones in his hands as he returned to the corridor. His foot hit a shovel on the way and it collapsed on the tools placed next to it, slamming into the door with a loud noise. Sisak ran up to help him, picked up the tools from the floor, arranged them next to the door, and replaced the shovel, examining its sharp edge as he did so. "I wonder if this is the same shovel that…" but he was scared that Harout could read his thoughts based on the way he was looking at the shovel, so he quickly said, "Your shovel seems to have gone blunt, you need to get it sharpened."

As Harout emptied his pockets of the eggs and placing them on the table, muttering, "How often do I need that shovel nowadays?"

Sisak cast another horrified look at the tool, recalling the day there had been a fight and Nakhshun's father Sargis had hit the door as he flew out, shaking the thick hinges.

"His neck… his neck… he'll chop off his neck. Come quick, please… help!" Old man Onés had placed a foot in the path of the sharp shovel that was coming at Sargis, and he was now weakly rolling on the floor and shouting in terror, "Everyone, come here… his neck… he'll chop off his neck!"

"He has no right to breathe the same air as me," Harout was grunting as he strained this way and that, trying to break free of the people who were holding him back, thinking that nothing would justify this defeat—neither the enemy's strength, nor one's own powerlessness, not even fate, which was God's will, "They did all this before his very eyes and he did nothing—he neither killed them, nor was he killed."

The villagers said, "Have pity on him."

Harout responded, "Whoever makes a sound will have their necks chopped off by this sharp shovel."

The virgin singer of the Arakelots Monastery in Mush had been raped on the road from Van to Erivan, and when they got to the village, her belly was already quite large. Harout had grabbed a shovel and lunged forward…

From the next day onward, Sargis lived outside the village, in the mountains—mountains? They were more like thorns stuck in the heel of the sky—and he moaned in terror there at night. Once or twice a month, Sargis tried to return but ended up facing Harout, that sharp shovel in his hand, ready to chop off his neck, or his bare hands itching to strangle him. "You'd moan too if the Turkish cavalry stormed into your house at night and trampled your fate with the hooves, crushing you in your bed," the villagers would tell him.

"No," Harout would respond, "He has no right to breathe the same air as me."

And Sargis would bitterly return to the mountains, where he would howl with the wolves.

The villagers would sometimes try to appeal to Harout's sense of pity. There were times when the howling of the pack would slam against the sky.

"One of those howls is coming from poor Sargis," a villager would say, his ears isolating the most mournful of those sounds.

"How do you know?" another one would cast doubt, "How could you identify Sargis in howling that is as confused as the wind?"

"A wolf's howls are hollow, but a human's howls hold hope."

But no matter what they said or how they tried to persuade him, Harout was unshakeable. Sato tried and tried to convince him. "Harout *jan*," she would say, "Every person's destiny has its own Turk to face, what good is it to drive him away?" And she would calm Nakhshun down, "Harout's heart is as pure as a pigeon's liver, his anger will subside and he'll forgive him." But nothing of the sort happened.

The migrants appreciated Harout's harsh stance. What they had seen was etched in their memory, they had polished their pain and crystallized it within themselves to the extent that they placed their lost homeland and their deceased family members in their teardrops. There were only sighs and fragmented words in their sobs, which also cursed the Kurds. "The Turks were devouring us, grabbing our land and our history. Why the Kurds joined their murderous campaign is beyond us."

Sargis was not a good wolf, his howls were unable to pierce the sky or go high enough. In order to cover up this mockery, the mountain wolves howled louder—owoo, owoo... Varso joined them, growling a rare word now and then... "Crucified... Crucified one by one."

"How did they crucify them, Varso? How?" the curious ones jumped in, "Like Christ? Or did they drive the nails in other parts of their body?"

"Oh," Varso would sigh and moan, arguing with God in her mind. "Oh God, wasn't there another way to save the world? Was everything really so corrupted that the only thing you could do was to come and use the cross?" And she would add out loud, "Why should I talk about these sad things and stain the blood in your veins? I should tell you a fairy tale instead."

Harout grabbed the eggs with his large fingers and put them in Sisak's lap.

"The life of an Armenian was equivalent to one gold piece in Der Zor. Parents would give the Janissaries a gold piece each, to keep their children from being raped and tortured to death, asking them to be shot dead instead... Here, meanwhile... twin Turks—twenty eggs. What a great deal," Sisak smirked when he looked at his face.

"Don't you dare..." Harout shouted. "Don't you dare use that word to describe the children. Nakhshun wouldn't be able to bear it. Those children must live, don't label them with that word, don't make it difficult for them to live here. They've already seen so much terror and humiliation before they were born, there's no need to add to that."

Sisak retreated in fear, then placed the eggs in his pockets and scolded Harout.

"Oh come on, brother... The concern you're showing for Nakhshun... I'm telling you, that guy, that poor migrant should come... What are you trying to do, anyway? You're wasting all your energy on these tormented folks, let that guy come and take care of his family..."

"No," Harout shouted, "Impossible. He has no right... That man should not step into this village."

"If Nakhshun has forgiven him, why are you making this so hard?"

"She can forgive him, but I won't. This is my village, he must not live here."

"Come on, what did he ever do to you?"

Harout slowly closed his eyelids, his heart still hot like the dying sun.

"Oh, I don't know… there are so many things that should be said, and left unsaid."

"Get that weight off your shoulders… Why are you creating trouble for yourself? The way you're behaving, people are saying that you have a thing for Nakhshun."

"I am a man that loves chastity. How can I have a thing for someone defiled by a Turk? Even the thought of heaven does not seduce me, because I know the Devil was once there."

In order to maintain order in the village, Harout would always roam about at night with his wolfhounds. They've seen him, standing there silently beneath Nakhshun's window, peeking in. Watching for hours as she moved about, undressed, ate, cried… Everyone knew it—the murky waters of spring had mixed with Harout's blood and they were corroding the banks as they flowed. Onés had even caught him once staring awestruck at Nakhshun when she had been bathing. "Son," he had said to Harout, feeling sorry for him, "She cannot love a man. This torment has eaten me up inside to the extent that my ears are now deaf to even the lullabies that my mother used to sing, but they still hear Nakhshun's screams as the Turkish and Kurdish men pulled her away from each other and to themselves. Leave her alone. She cannot love a man anymore." There had been silence for a moment. It had been Onés who broke it with a sigh. "I don't know what the Heavenly One is thinking when He gives human beings pain like this… The force of this pain has changed how my soul is built." Harout had looked at him.

"Had she really been a singer?" He had asked, his voice as indifferent as he could make it sound.

"Oh, and *what* a singer she had been," Onés has moaned, "It was like she could dip her voice in your blood."

"Get that weight off your shoulders…" Sisak continued to persuade him, "Let that man come and be the head of his family."

"Impossible."

"You wouldn't be saying that if you had a family and children."

"What is this? Does the world need fresh blood to drink, does it need fresh flesh to chew? No way… Can someone who has seen so much trust the world enough to bring a new generation into it? I would rather take my blood back with me, I'm sure God could make use of it somewhere. My name will go on, they've named little Harout after me, that's the important thing."

[32]

Sisak was quiet for a moment, then he went on the offensive.

"They've seen her come to your house... Nakhshun, I mean."

"Yes, she may have come a couple of times. She brought a pillow one time, and a bedsheet the other... She thinks she's still among the Turks, she wants to mollify me with presents."

"Yes indeed, a pillow and sheet. Did I say it had been something else? That's how it always starts. A pillow, then a sheet... and then... They're not going to leave that bed empty... they're going to come and make sure it's occupied."

"Get the hell out of here, you..." Harout lunged forward, standing on the leg that hurt.

Sisak, startled and offended, slammed the door shut as he fled. He went to pay off Sato, who was drunk and tired when she left the woman who had given birth. She breathed out a mix of vodka and garlic, her tired eyes blinking beneath her curly, confused brows, and said with pride, "That one, the first one that came... oh... it was a mature baby, looked right at me as if to say 'I'm here, kill me.' The second one, oh, I felt so sorry for it, it looked so innocent... so innocent, that it was a sin—so innocent that it is no longer a virtue, but a fault. In any case... my price is the same, thirty eggs."

Three days later, when Sato had seemed to calm down and nobody in the village was being born or dying, she walked to Harout's house. Harout had placed a pot on the wood furnace and was roasting the trout fish with wheat. The fire in the furnace was strong, the wood crackled as the flames struck the walls.

"Good morning," Sato sat down next to the furnace, softening with the heat and watching the red grains of wheat sizzle, wet with their fear of the heat, pop into each other in the air and then fall back into the pot.

"Morning," Harout picked up a plate from the wooden table that already had some cold roasted wheat on it, and he placed it in front of Sato.

"I took out her womb and disposed with all of it," Sato spoke, without mentioning a name, with no introduction, as if continuing a previous conversation left unfinished.

"Why?"

"It was damaged."

"You should have treated it—isn't that your job?"

"I didn't know if I could."

[33]

"Don't tell her," Harout sighed.

"I wouldn't have told you either, if I wasn't scared that…" Sato got up, walked to the wooden bucket near the door, used two fingers to pick out a fly that had drowned in the sticky yoghurt drink, stuck in a clay cup, and held it out to Harout as it dripped from the sides.

"Have some *than.*"[4]

"You were scared that…"

"Scared that you would marry her… Who needs a man without an heir?"

At that moment, three boys walked past Harout's house, grabbing a piece of *gata* from each other's hands, shoving each other about and laughing.

"I wonder which of these three is yours," Sato indicated the children and tried some humor to pacify Harout.

"Why would I have anything in common with these children?" Harout said awkwardly.

"Come on… You played so many games of hide-and-seek with their mother in the hayfields… Whatever you say, I think the middle one has your eyes."

"Enough of that, now…"

The only other people to have gone through the village like that were the Arabs, four hundred years ago. But, to their credit, they had not killed the desire to live. They had left some ruins behind where, until the Armenian Genocide of 1896, all kinds of snakes would live, and the life of a snake is still a life, it is the work of the Creator. Mnik's grave had also remained, where Perch had unknowingly taken a seat when he had reached the highest peak, and the world had come to an end in the bony snow of the summit… Mnik's grave, the only evidence of earlier life in the village, had a simple image on it; a small circle—his head, a large circle—his bloated belly, the lines emerging at its sides—his arms and legs, a *saz*[5] placed on his abdomen—he had probably played the *saz*—and a date etched into it—1666, with the writing, "Here rests Mnik, who died at the hands of the lawless…" Nobody knew who the lawless had been; it could be anyone—so many people had come and gone in this world… In any case, there had been life,

4   A drink made of watered-down yoghurt.
5   A stringed instrument also called *bağlama* in some countries.

so Harout and Perch brought resurrection to the village. And when the new migrants had barely managed to escape the genocide of 1915, Harout—who had migrated in 1896 from Latar and started a village on the ruins left by the Arabs—was already a local, although his family tree here had started with him and had not born any fruit with other names.

There was no church dome here, no rows of cross-stones in a cemetery, their shadows did not stretch with the light of the sunset. There were no walls or fences that set the boundaries of life... People here would slip through the rocks like lizards, lived in concealment and nourished themselves with ground water. No cross, no churches or priests—they had seen so many burning churches, smashed crosses and massacred clergymen that they no longer had a place for God except to hold Him within themselves and in ciphered prayers, with no particular interest in the true path to a polished heaven.

Nobody knew where the village had been, it was as if time itself was scared to go there because the jagged rocks would cut into it, for even a meticulous search would not reveal anything that could be further reduced to dust—the mountains were too big for that. The village did not grow through the number of births in it, but through the number of times that Harout left to go into the world outside. He would always find someone who seemed lost, someone making an escape—from the law, the Turks, from a woman, from one's own self... When he got to the village, Harout would first remove the straw that he used to cover the rock salt from the sun, then he would take out the gray pieces of rock salt, and help out someone from beneath them, someone to whom he had given a long explanation on the way there—"Nobody cares what you've done or who you were. Here, you have been a decent human being and live a decent life. Otherwise, I'll take you back in the same cart with your eyes blindfolded, placing you beneath the pickled fish, and I'll drop you off where I picked you up." Nobody would ask the newcomer any unnecessary questions. "You don't ask people questions when they're standing beneath the ruins of their destiny." Everyone was free to make up their own life story here, to edit their past lives or embellish them... The village had another advantage—it was like a cemetery. Once you went it, you did not come out. Only Harout knew the way into the village and the way out. He would set out for the world outside several times a year... as Perch would do before him. He had kept the path to the outside world a secret from everyone until Harout had grown older. Harout inherited that path from him because they had lived together in the times of their escape. Of course, there had been a moment, when Perch was still alive, that they had decided to reveal themselves, to tell the world they existed, but after 1896 came 1905, and then 1915… There had never been more blood and tragedy than in those years. And they were glad that they had not made that foolish error, that there was a place where they could hide from the pursuits of life. "Never let the world meddle in your life," Perch had told him, "Never…"

But, nevertheless, the world meddled.

Nakhshun—the villagers called the pregnant woman by this name meaning "beauty" a month after she had rid herself of her rags, taken a bath and had normal meals, when she had gained weight and the villagers had seen that the Turks and Kurds were not just capable of cruelty but also possessed a sense of taste. She was a beauty indeed—with white skin, a sleek body, and she seemed to have no bones, like a snake. The woman gladly accepted her new name, leaving the old one with her ordeals in the desert of Der Zor. But alas, the howling that often came down from the mountains and the child bouncing in her belly would sometimes deal her consciousness a swift kick.

She would rarely leave the house because, although people would whisper with pity and forgiveness, "It's unfortunate… what can the poor woman do?" they would keep casting curious glances at her belly. And she fumbled around under her apron helplessly, twisting and bending her fingers to the extent that it caused her pain…

Nakhshun bore her pregnancy proudly even though she felt the looks and pity that people hurled at her belly, and her ears picked up the judgmental gossip around her. For example, what gave those two widows, that disgusting Margush and that crusty Gyulnar, the right to gossip about her during Argam's son's engagement? Margush had come to the village at Harout's heels, holding the hands of her two children and it had only been this year when a poisonous green snake had bitten her as she collected wood in the mountains and the women had rushed her to the village as she burned with fever, hurrying to keep her alive, that she had started to blab deliriously about how she had left her three elder children behind and fled the house with only the two younger ones. Gyulnar's husband was sitting on a donkey and crossing along the edge of the gorge when the evil spirits descended at once, drove the animal crazy, and it went off the path and straight into the abyss below... Once again, may God grant Harout a long life, he had tied his horsehair rope to his waist and pulled the man out... All his bones were broken, but at least he had a grave of his own, he did not end up as prey to the wild animals. And these two widows, Margush stuffing the *gata* with sweet filling into her cheek, Gyulnar chewing on some roasted wheat, were staring right at Nakhshun's belly—they could have at least thought of looking elsewhere so that she would not be able to guess their thoughts—as they whispered furiously into each other's ear.

"There is some good fortune in misery as well... Our children may be fatherless, but at least they know their lineage on that side. Can you imagine having children like her?"

"Oh, God forbid... May such remain far from our homes..." and she spat three times into her bosom as was the custom to ward off the evil eye. And fragments of their conversation, purposefully pronounced loudly, reached Nakhshun's ears...

"And what about the man she's with now? Imagine being with a person who's forcing your father to howl like a wolf! Yuk, disgusting," and Gyulnar bit into the *gata* she was holding with such savagery that one would have expected it to start bleeding.

"Harout's not like that," said Bero, her eyes fixated on Nakhshun but also seemingly checking whether or not she could hear them, "He's probably taken her father somewhere else by now... Howling? Only nothingness can survive the cold in those mountains, would he even be able to gather the air in his lungs to howl?"

Nakhshun pretended not to notice or, rather, she was afraid that within another sentence or two she would be declared a leper like Job the Blessed, and the world would be warned that she had been defiled, that everyone should stay away from her for fear of being infected. But then Maro jumped in—the same Maro that had paid Sato with a silver ring instead of eggs, the same Maro that had aborted her baby and continued her relationship with her sister's husband five minutes later. She looked Nakhshun up and down, seeing her wearing a woolen dress with laces that she had made herself, and said,

"She's a pretty woman," as if it was not Nakhshun that she was talking about, as if she was not in the room, as if she was absent. Then she added, as if to herself, but within earshot of everyone, "But damn that Harout, he's got such a head on his shoulders... would he do something if it was going to harm him?"

And she turned towards Nakhshun and spewed out, "Harout is doing a good job of taking care of you." But then she saw her go red and freeze in place, and she regretted her actions somewhat. "Although," she added, "There's no need for this gossip. I wouldn't call it love. It's just that our Harout is like God—he stands by everyone who has been raped and is in misery." She said this and held her neck straight with triumph.

Nakhshun could not hold back any longer.

"Yes," she said, trembling with fear, "And because you are a virgin like death, instead of being raped like life itself, the appearance of God does not bother you."

When Harout caught wind of this story, he thought, "Wow..." and was happy at Nakhshun's rebellion, "So there is some life in her yet." At that point, Nakhshun had turned towards Varso and recalled the advice she had given her, "Rub coal dust on your face, rub coal... let them think you are as black as they are..." She picked up a piece of *halva* from the table and placed it in front of Varso.

"Varso *jan*... why aren't you eating anything?"

Varso had lived in a city and owned a pastry shop. She used to bake the type of baklava called "the lady's navel" with threads of flour so thin they would go through the eye of a needle, and she would mix almonds and walnuts with honey and oriental spices as well as the sweetness of her own fingers, doing everything she could to make the treat live up to its name and so that whoever ate it would feel the same pleasure as someone kissing a lady's navel. And now she had ended up in a place where dough dipped in oil—halva with sugar water—was considered the grandest of things. What was poor Varso to do? Neither the truth could help in such a situation, nor a lie. So she would escape and hide behind her story.

"What would you do? The prince's horse twisted its ankle in the forest, so I bandaged it. If it gets better, that's good, otherwise we'll kill it. But the king's poor son... how is the prince supposed to walk all the way back?

Look at how sunny it is," and she stuck her hand out in an aggressive gesture at the sky that had mellowed in the heat.

Varso had been provided the village with its biggest shock. They had seen many migrants and Turks—after all, was there a Christian out there whose fate had not been sliced by the *yataghan*?—but it was the first time they had seen a woman that smoked. Varso would smoke whatever she could find— tobacco, cannabis, tree bark, grass… She would stuff it into her wooden pipe and puff away. Then she would inhale it all with a deep breath, filling her heart and lungs with the smoke, allowing it to penetrate into each cell before releasing the enriched fumes in clouds through her nostrils.

At first, the children had been afraid of her. But Varso had managed to win over the village within a week. Her story began very beautifully—"the red, southeastern wind awoke in the mother's belly… It swallowed the hills and fields in its path, buckled the river around its waist like a belt, kicked aside a mountain and uprooted it, and walked up to the sky… it grabbed the soul of the sky in its fist and shook it hard. The villagers ran to cover up their haystacks so that the wind would not blow them away, they dragged their animals indoors to keep them from drowning in the rain and what did they see? The king's middle son stood in the doorway, riding his fiery steed…" Not yet fully awake, without a bite of breakfast, the children would run over to Varso's in the morning to hear the rest of the story. "The king's son was brushing the horse's mane," Varso would tell them, continuing to smoke, "Again? How many days can you brush a horse's mane?" the children would be surprised. "You shouldn't rush ahead," Varso would say, "The king's son did not hurry, he had lots of time." And the children would leave only to come back the following day and hear the continuation. It was one story, but it took a long time to tell, and Varso spent a whole lifetime narrating it. She appeared in the village when she was a woman past fifty, she died at the threshold of a hundred or slightly past it, still elaborating the same story. She even managed to turn it into a weapon—she would send one of the children to gather some water, "Go get some water so I can continue," or "Until you dry my grass into hay, the king's son will remain stranded in the swamp." The children were not naïve, but they realized that if Varso could continue telling stories even after living such a long life, they had no choice—they quietly carried out her orders. And this excited Varso even more.

"The king's son stood there, and three paths lay before him—one to the right, one to the left, and straight ahead. He went straight… He went a long way, or perhaps a short one, but ended up stranded in a swamp," and at this point, she would fall asleep.

"Well?" the children would nudge her, "What happened next?"

"Next? The king of the swamp invited him to a feast and the prince lay down to rest in the Garden of Eden. You can go home now, he's very tired, he will sleep till tomorrow. Bring me some cheese, otherwise the king of the swamp may poison the food that he gives the prince, and that handsome young man will die because of you…"

"We can bring some wine too. Perhaps that monster can have some and fall asleep…"

"If the monster has some and falls asleep, who's going to tell the story? Just bring some cheese, that's enough."

The children would come the following day and find out that the king's son had woken early and regretted his earlier decision, and had now taken the path to the right. "He went down the path and… ended up stuck in a swamp."

"Are there swamps everywhere he goes?" the children were incredulous.

"Yes," Varso would sigh. "Whether you go to the right, or to the left, even if you fly straight up or down. You can go any way you want—in the end, life is a swamp. It swallows you up and chews your bones before digesting you."

But there was, nevertheless, a difference. The monster in the swamp on the right side swallowed the young prince. Five minutes later, the king's son was riding his horse on the path to the left.

"He managed to escape the belly of the beast? How?" the children's eyes shimmered with surprise and awe.

"By the grace of God."

"But is that possible? The monster had not coughed, or sneezed, or yawned… It never opened its mouth. It didn't even burp… How did he get out of there?"

"Come on, kids," Varso was already getting irritated at the children's stubborn questions, "God has managed to rescue Varso from the clutches of the Turks, what difficulty would it pose to tear open the belly of a monster and rescue the king's son? And the young prince had a fiery sword in his hand, after all…"

Anything new came to the village through one of three paths, just like the choices faced by the king's son in the story—straight, right, and left. It happened either when a child was born in the village, when Harout went out into the world and returned to tell the people what he had seen, or through Varso's story.

The migrants were supplying Nakhshun with whatever they could manage to find—meat, fruits, *gata*. They would slip it into her lap and say, "Eat this... when the baby is born, name him after my son, blessed child..." They would cry bitterly when they looked at her belly, "What could you say, what could you ask? Oh God, wipe that from my memory, from your own memory, erase it from the memory of the world... That kind of pain must not be given the right to exist even as a memory."

The migrants had saved their family members from the massacres only in the form of memories, and they would only communicate with each other through their lamentations and dreams.

They were trying to breathe life into the dead at any cost—by passing on their names to others, by giving gifts on their birthdays to someone else of approximately the same age, by distributing their share of sweets by the fistful—a handful for each dead family member—to their fellow villagers on the memorial day for the deceased... This would usually begin at noon. A group of mourning women would appear on the street and the one walking in front would have a plate full of sweets. Sometimes, different groups would form at each end of the street, or simultaneously on several streets. The locals would walk toward the cemetery to smoke incense at their relative's gravesite, mourn, and commune with his or her soul. The migrants had no such good fortune—their relatives were graveless, and they would do several rounds of the village streets, until the plate no longer held any sweets, and their hearts no longer held any tears. The woman walking in front would examine the yards, the curb, the depths of the residential land and, as soon as she spotted someone, she would throw a handful of sweets in his or her direction, whispering inaudibly, "This is for my mother... This is for my brother... This is for my son..." They would pronounce the names of the dead in their minds in order to avoid scaring the children, so as to prevent a conflict between the living and the dead.

[41]

At first, the children would shudder at the sight of this procession for the dead. Then, a few brave ones among them would gather the sweets spread out on the ground or catch them mid-air... they would raise this portion for the deceased to their mouths with apprehension, feel the sweetness as they bit into it, then jump up to catch the second handful. In the end, the children would be nauseated from eating too many sweets. After the people left, the ground would be covered in hard candy, *gata* and *halva*, as well as pieces of crystallized sugar... They had gone, leaving behind these sweet items, while other destinies remained that needed to be lived out and exhausted, so that their lives would have meaning. The dead were many, the living were few, the villagers could not eat all the sweets, no matter how much they wanted to...

"If it's a boy, give him my father's name or my brother's... The Turks consumed their souls, but may their names live on." Yeran had a different way of making this request compared to the others—her words were accompanied by generosity. She would cook something tasty every day and bring over a lot of it. This had escalated to robbery at some point—not a day went by without a fight between her and her husband. It would often happen that he would flip the salted wolf's hide this way and that on the stones under the wall and Hako would ask with a quiet anger, "Where's the fish?"

"The cat got it, that damn thing..." Yeran would whine, evasively.

Hako would be persistent.

"I asked you a question—where's the fish?"

"Well, you should put it in a place where the cat can't reach," one of the neighbors would jump in from the other side of the fence in order to keep Hako in control so that he would not hit his wife, "Not even a snake can catch a cat with a fish, can it? And what good is a cat that has had its fill to eat?"

"This is the real snake," Hako would say, pointing to Yeran. "This woman is a thief! Wife, where's the fish?"

"The cat ate it," Yeran would sob.

"Take off your clothes," Hako would shout, tugging at his wife's ample skirt with its many folds, "You've hidden it in your skirt somewhere."

"The cat ate it," Yeran would cry, gathering her skirt around herself.

"Hako *jan*, a man shouldn't fight over food," the neighbor once again made her presence felt.

[42]

"But this woman is a thief," Hako would shout, offended by his own revelation, tugging at his wife, "One day it's the chicken, the next day it's the butter, then the cheese… She's robbing the house, mouthful by mouthful… Take off your clothes, I say… I'll find that fish in the folds of your skirt right now. Damn your skirt… It hides all kinds of ugly things," and he would pull at it again.

Yeran would scream and cry helplessly.

"There's no other way, I'm going to go and drown myself in Lake Sevan."

During their last fight, an angel came and settled next to Yeran's head… A thick wire running through the heads of several oily fish thumped to the ground, and the dust they kicked up rose to Hako's knees.

"Here's your fish," Harout shouted, "Leave this woman alone,"

Hako stared at the large whitefish that Harout had brought, his eyes cold and mucous in the dust.

"The fish is not the point. She's a thief, you understand? A thief!"

"Come on," the women on the other side of the fence whispered to each other, "You've come to own some property after all those hardships. Why steal now?"

Harout looked threateningly at Hako.

"This isn't my fish. Mine was a two-kilogram trout…"

"Shame on you… she was hungry, she must have eaten it."

Yeran interrupted them, sobbing.

"I stick to what I was saying. The cat ate it."

"Heard that?" Harout picked up the soil-covered oily fish from the ground wrapped the fire running through the fish around Hako's neck. "Go back inside, I don't want to hear another word from you. The cat ate it—understood?"

Hako reddened at the dishonesty and ran inside angrily, the wire with the fish still around his neck; he grabbed a net and scale, then stepped outside again.

"The cat…" he mumbled, livid, looking around the yard, "The cat ate it, did it?" Then he noticed the cat's tail sticking out from behind the door and dragged it out, holding up the light-haired, young cat in the air. The cat showed no surprise and tried to paw the fish hanging around Hako's neck, as he dropped it into the net and weighed it.

"There you go," he said, bringing the scales closer for Harout to see, "Two kilograms… That's my fish, then… but where's the cat?" And he left, cursing

[43]

ferociously… his arms waving at his sides as if in conversation with someone, he spoke loudly and swore. He stopped only at one spot to remove a small stone from his shoe, then continued in the same way as he blended into the dusk.

Yeran sat there, crying and staring. The calf tied to the fence wanted to chew at the nettles. It extended its mouth but the nettle stung it, so it grunted and moved its head aside. It extended its mouth again but the nettle would not give up and stung it again. The calf shook its ears and grunted… this time, it brought its mouth closer at a side angle… Yeran patiently watched the battle between the calf and the nettle until the street emptied, the people forgot her and the fish, and returned to their chores. She wiped her wet eyes and nose with her apron. She looked left and right to make sure that there was nobody around. She ran up to the nettle, ripped it out of the ground and threw it aside. The calf now wanted a taste of its roots and sniffed at the soiled, wet radix. Yeran quickly dug up the soil, removed the fish wrapped in paper, put in down her waist into her ample skirt and rushed out the fence, her dream burning brightly.

"Eat this," she said to Nakhshun, putting the fish on the table. "Eat this, so your child is healthy."

The "Turks"—that is what the whole village christened the migrants after the twins were born, even though the immigrant women had married the local men and borne children, even though the elderly men that had come with them had married the local widows. The neighborhood where they lived was still called the Turks' district.

When the children turned forty days old, Nakhshun distributed *halva* and *gata* with saccharine filling, so that her daughters would only see sweetness in their lives. "How strange!" the children of the neighborhood were surprised, "This is the same *gata* and *halva* that they give out on the memorial day for the dead."

"They have lived among foreigners," their mothers explained, "They see no particular difference between life and death… Eat it, eat it all. The stomach does not discriminate."

Nakhshun's twins proved to be a determined lot. They snorted about for three months, developed a fever and did not eat, they whined day and night helplessly… but they did not die. They lived. Once again, it was Sato that saved them. They had been born in fear—they could not tell the difference between darkness and light. They did not sleep, play or eat breastmilk like other babies. On the third day, when Sato realized that their hearts could explode with their screams, she decided to pour some wax. She did not even tell their mother of her intentions. When she came over to bathe the newborns, she quietly slipped the children's dirty clothes into her bosom and left. She removed them at home, put them beneath a silver cross, read out a prayer, then held a pot with water beneath a candle and poured wax into it. The hot drops fell into the cold water and hissed, destroying the curse that was clinging to the children. When the next day arrived, she brought back the clothes on which she had prayed, and slipped them back in the same way, planning to put them on the children. But she saw that the twins were screaming just like the previous day, and Nakhshun's nipples had cracked and were raw, like ripe pomegranates. There was no other way. "If it were only your nipples, I'd put some wheat kneaded with honey on them and they'd get better, but the evil eye is on you," she said, "I have to pour lead on you."

Nakhshun laughed in disbelief. "Why would the evil eye be on me? Did I have any good fortune that it could take from me? Could anyone possibly be envious of me?"

"Don't say crazy things," Sato cut her off, "Others take a pilgrimage and honor seven saints just to have one child. God has blessed you with two, just like that."

"Oh really? Just like that?" Nakhshun thought, offended. But she got out of bed, and obediently sat down. Sato brought the swaddled babies to her and placed them tightly beside her, as if planning to make sure they would all fit beneath the clay pot she was now holding. She dipped her fingers in the cold water and flicked a few drops here and there.

"What do you smell?" she asked and dictated her response, "Say 'roses and violets.'"

"Roses and violets," Nakhshun repeated.

"What do you see before your eyes?" and once again, she dictated her response in a whisper, "The army of my guardian angels."

"The army of my guardian angels," Nakhshun repeated obediently.

"Good, very good," Sato grew excited, "The smell of roses and violets is everywhere, and God is with us through the army of guardian angels." She gave Nakhshun the pot and got busy. She put a piece of lead in a clay spoon, then removed a piece of charcoal from the furnace and put it on the edge of the *tonir*. "Don't say a word," she ordered Nakhshun and put the spoon on it. She watched the smoke rising and said a prayer until the lead melted. Then she picked up the spoon and took the pot from the other woman's hand. Then she held the pot over Nakhshun's head and poured the molten lead into the water in the pot. "Oh dear, oh dear... Phooey..." she spat in fear as she looked in the pot. Then she picked up the hardened lead with two fingers and held it before Nakhshun's eyes. "Do you see it?" she asked mysteriously, as if the misshapen piece of lead was an obvious clue. She wrapped the lead with a seven-colored thread and put it in her pocket, after which she gave the mother a sip of the water to drink and flicked a drop carefully on the newborns. "That's all," she said with self-satisfaction, "Now we're done with the curse." She was trying to convince herself first of all, as she picked up the rest of the water and poured it beneath the roseship bush.

When she came back in, she was followed by Yeran, who was holding some roasted grain. She placed the dish of sweet roasted grain, the fat cooling on it, next to Nakhshun's bed and insisted, "Eat this, so you have milk."

Nakhshun thought to herself as she ate the warm roasted grain, "I wonder if she took a beating for this, or if she managed to make up a decent lie." The next thought that came from Yeran's presence was about the children's names. Throughout her pregnancy, everyone had given her the best food as compensation for reviving the names of their family members. When the girls were born, she knew she was going to name them after her mother and paternal aunt, but how could she bestow a name upon them that had lived for ten generations and then burned at the hands of the Turks? So she made up a lie.

"I saw St. Sargis in a dream last night. He came and whispered the names of two of our ancient goddesses—Astghik and Anahit."

"Hmph," Yeran did not agree with the saint, "If our ancient gods had any power left in them, Christ would not have been able to draw the people away from them." She was upset that the twins were girls, which meant that nobody would claim her father's and uncle's names. Yeran grunted, then crossed herself in fear, "I bow before that holy power."

"Is this what Christ's power is capable of?" Sato indicated the two swaddled things lying next to each other.

"Did you see it?" Yeran slapped a hand against her knee, encouraged at what Sato had just said. "Sato *jan*, did you see what happened?"

"What happened?" Sato looked at her in fear.

"What else could have happened? The twins were born girls—nobody was left to claim my father's and uncle's names."

"So maybe you should try having a boy yourself," Sato joked and stepped outside. On her way home, she threw the piece of lead and the string into the river. "Take it away," she told the flowing water, "Take away the pain and misery from those poor things."

Encouraged by what Sato had said, Yeran was convinced that she would be the one to revive the name that had been lost in her family, because every person has a purpose in life and a name to revive. And she found a way to do it. She went to gather grass and was pregnant when she returned, she went to harvest vegetables and was pregnant when she returned. Her womb bore boys on four occasions and they were all named Garnik, but each of them would die on the third or fourth day, and when she bore the last one, whom she had brought from the fields where she had gone to collect thyme, she took him and dropped him off at Vazgen's wife's place, who was also expecting a boy in those days. She said, "I've seen so much horror that my blood has changed its composition and has turned to water. That is why my children are dying. Put your child's clothes on mine, give him your milk to drink." And the child lived. He was mute, despite the fact that they hung a key blessed in church on a seven-colored thread around his neck till the end of his life, hoping that it would unlock the power of speech for him. And for so many years, Harout would take that silver key with him when he went out into the world, visiting all the churches on his way and asking them to bless it with prayers before he brought it back. There were no churches left unvisited in Armenia, the key even went to some of them three or four times… Twice a day, at sunrise and sunset, they would twist the key near his mouth, like one would do when opening a padlock. One part of the key had bent from use, the other had grown thin, but the lock on his tongue remained firm as ever and did not relent. "That name brought bad luck," people concluded, and nobody gave that name to any of their children for another hundred years in that village, until a century had rolled past and the name had been purified.

Yeran was not one to give up on her objectives. She would have had more children, but a bear broke her husband and turned him into a handful of flesh. When Harout came down from the mountains half-conscious, carrying Hako on his back, the villagers rushed forward to help him and Yeran was among them, wailing that she would no longer be able to convince her green-eyed husband to ignore the gossip, jealousy and malice, and believe that the child was his. Hako was overcome with emotion when he saw the flood of tears Yeran was shedding for him, and managed to joke even in his half-dead state, "Don't cry, Yero *jan*, the bear hasn't touched the part of me that you're entitled to. That part is intact and undamaged. But when Sato spent a sweat-drenched month treating him and he saw no improvement—Hako had no sensation below his armpits—he suddenly grew more miserable. He would call out several times a day, "Yero, oh Yero, how I love you…" Yeran would listen tensely, hoping that the second half of the sentence would be different this time, but as soon as she heard another "How I love you…" she would strike her knees in angst. "Oh, he's soiled himself again." She would change him and come back, looking at her hands—red, the skin cracked and swollen from doing the laundry and carrying heavy loads—and raising them in protest at her misfortune, "Dear God, we managed to escape the Turks through some miracle, but what have you brought upon us instead? There is no option to escape, yet there is no way to stay…What can I do? Oh God!"

Harout had connected his cart to his oxen in those days and set off for Yerevan, loaded with incense collected from trees, salted fish, three dried sheepskins, one fox fur with the eyes and paws still intact, which he planned to exchange for sugar and chintz cloth. As soon as he had returned, he rushed to Sato for a verification of the news that he had picked up. Sato had just finished baking bread and was crushing the fresh loaf into some yellow fat as it crackled on the fire, she was preparing to eat *chmur*. The pieces of hot bread had melted the fat and absorbed it, swelling like hail-bearing clouds. She offered some to Harout as well. Harout licked the warm fat off his fingers as he ate, then he asked,

"Is it true that you were assaulted?"

"Yes, the women beat me up… They asked me why I was caring for them, why I didn't let them die. They haven't been taking milk, bread and water for so many days, saying that they should die. Why should we feed the Turks and raise them?"

"What did you say?"

"What would I say? I'm me. What do I care what others say?"

"So help them, get those children on their feet."

"But what if they're right? What if the two of us are wrong when it comes to these children and how we feel sorry for them and love them? They are children today and we take pity on them, but when they grow up, they will be Turks and they will slaughter us."

"Yes," Harout burst out, "I am always wrong—whether we're talking about the children, or when it comes to enemies, friends, life, and death… The only case in which I've never been wrong is when it comes to God, and that is more than enough to keep me alive… So, know this, Sato—if anything happens to those children, my horsehair rope is ready for action."

After that, Harout would demonstratively pluck a hair from his horse's tail every day, then he would sit in his yard at the end of the week and weave the hairs together into a rope, which he would tighten around his waist instead of a belt when he dropped off a loaf of bread at Nakhshun's porch before leaving. Little Harout would come along, waving another horsehair in the air and asking him to teach him how to weave a rope.

"You're still too small," Harout would reply.

"Weaving a rope is not such a tough thing, why do I need to grow up for it?"

"The weaving part is not hard, what's difficult is forcing yourself to keep from using what you've woven."

The rejected little Harout would rush off, upset, to listen to the day's story.

"Varso, tell me the truth. Which horse is stronger—Harout's or the prince's?"

"No…" Varso would stretch out the word confidently, "I hope the king's son will forgive me for saying this, but his horse needs to eat a lot more hay to be able to match Harout's. There is only one Harout in this world, just as there is only one Wild Horse."

Harout continued bringing them bread for a long time, ignoring the gossip and innuendos, as well as the silent muttering to themselves of the people. Throughout that time, he spoke to Nakhshun only once, when he had already placed the loaf of bread at her door, on the rock which the animals would lick for salt, and knocked on the window softly to let her know that she could pick it up, and she had rushed out to Sato's to pick up a potion that would loosen her children's bowels.

Harout looked her over.

"Are you good?"

"I can't get used to it," Nakhshun complained, upset with herself, her sad eyes drooping but not telling him that everything in that house seemed to her like a harbinger of death. She had been gripped by postnatal depression and the delusions would not release her. Everything inspired a sense of fear within her. The moon looked like a *yataghan* that was going to rip the belly of the sky open, the clouds were dripping with gloom, the darkness was poking the sky in the eyes and the stars were going blind one after the other, the howling wind would seem like a human cry to her… The wet throes of the wind on the lake would blow cold misery from its nonexistent lungs on to the shore, and the frozen sand would shudder… Based on whether the wind was coming from the mountains or the lake, she would breathe differently, but the air coming to her would bring her the same—mourning and lamentations. The sun… that piece of gold had abandoned her in the hour of her greatest need. At night, the wind would rise up into the sky and struck its back to the invisible ceiling, shattering and shaking it. She had known for sure that it was the wind, but somehow she thought that in that way, like that day, the Turk soldiers of the desert were shaking the ground with their galloping and their laughter.

The desert trembled under Sargis Agha's feet and it seemed like he would fall flat on his face at any moment and be swallowed by the sand. But even the bone-melting sand could not stop him from moving. He swayed as he walked, somehow reining in the crumbling sand beneath his feet, his gaze frozen at the horsemen before him. He finally reached them and held out the gold, telling them what he needed in return. One of the horsemen took the gold, turned it this way and that to examine it, and then nodded his head with satisfaction in response—yes. Even at that calamitous moment, Sargis Agha's actions inspired respect among the migrants. His elder daughter was convinced that the possibility to buy one's death was a discovery her father had made, and it spread like a virus, with everyone using it as the only way to escape the inevitable. Like a real man, Sargis Agha made no pleas or shed no tears as he struck the deal with the bandits—the gold, the girl that was breaking ranks and running, the bullet. The gold—the bullet, the gold—the bullet... He was certain that all his children had been killed, saved from pain and dishonor. He had probably thought long and hard about it, it had probably occurred to him at the very beginning. Had he thought about or considered whether their mother would survive the children's death, or would the children be able to bear their mother's... In any case, he acted as if he had been distributing sweets—first to the little ones, the little ones must remain innocent, life must not lose its value in their eyes to that extent, they must die in naiveté. And they started with the little ones—his one-and-a-half-year-old son, whom he had dressed in girl's clothes. Sargis went and stood near the horse's legs and called the child to him tenderly. The child ran forward when his father spoke... One bullet. Sargis Agha grabbed his ears and fell to his knees. The thumping of the child to the ground had been so insignificant that it had caused no impact except for lifting the sand beneath the body and spraying it on his living sisters' feet. The eldest sister looked down at her feet and the sand that was burning them. Did any of them scream or cry? It seemed like they did not. After the first four, the mother of the family lost consciousness. She fell in the sand right in front of her daughter. The person firing the bullets showed some humanity and fired, eventually... As the deal was being carried out, this was the only case when he fired first and received the gold later.

Judging from the fact that Sargis Agha and the Turk were talking to each other without swearing, they probably knew each other, and the Turk was still displaying the respect he had held for the man. He not only allowed him to bury the dead, he agreed to kill the final two only after they had finished burying the rest. And when Sargis Agha's relative approached next, he used the same word—Agha—to address the man, who was bedraggled and diminished by torment. He had been the one who had directed the group of bandits, and the elder daughter was certain that she had been right—her father had known them. The relative could do nothing to help, of course, but found the humanity within himself to look the other way...

The last two that remained were Sargis Agha and his eldest daughter. They began to bury their family members. The sand was soft, it did not resist like soil, and was easy to dig, even though it burned and was very unstable, immediately slipping back into the hole that had been dug and filling it. When they approached the mother and turned her body over, she moaned.

She was not dead. The daughter spoke to her. There was no reply, not even a faint moan. Had she heard all the shots, she wondered? She must have felt the ground moving as each of her children fell—the sand was unstable and there were air particles between the grains, and air would conduct the vibrations along the ground… The daughter was surprised at her mother's stubbornness—what had kept her alive after seeing the death of her children, why did she cling to life like this and refuse to die?

When Sargis Agha's trembling fingers removed the bullet from his living wife's chest so that she could bleed freely and die, allowing them to bury her before moving on, the black blood flowed from the mother's white chest… One of the Turks laughed and said with a smile, "The old man is collecting more gold."

They whipped them—hurry up, get it over … No need to dig deep holes… We're not going to stand around and wait here because of you… But the wife would not die even though she had lost so much blood. Sargis Agha was forced to give more gold. His wife's death had cost him two gold pieces. The looks in the eyes of the bandits gave the daughter goosebumps and for a moment she considered snatching the gold from her father's hand—that was supposed to buy her death, after all. But the Turk had already grabbed it and was biting it to check whether it was a fake.

The daughter held a grudge against her mother that lasted forever. Why had she stolen my share of bullets? When she had given her life, she had held nothing back from her—health, intelligence, beauty… She had kept nothing for herself, she had given it all to her daughter. But now, before dying, she had shown some greed, grabbing her share of bullets and not allowing her the death to which she was entitled.

The Turks would later express amazement at how the old Armenian had managed to hide three gold pieces in his rags. It had been enough for everyone; he had just been short two gold pieces—one for his eldest daughter and one for himself…

"Take them out," the next group of Turks shouted angrily as their horses trampled on Sargis and they pulled his elder daughter this way and that. "Take out all the gold."

Sargis Agha had cast aside his feeling of shame and was crying, rubbing his face against the hot sand.

"You can see I'm naked, I have no more gold…"

"Take it out…" they shouted, "You're an Armenian. No Armenian moves about without gold, you must have hidden it somewhere… There are all kinds of places you can hide gold in your body. Think again… a naked Armenian must have at least three handfuls of gold concealed somewhere…" and they kept beating him.

Nakhshun had no idea what her face had revealed when she said, "I can't get used to it," because Harout had the following advice,

"Forget it… Forget it all, don't torment yourself or your poor children… You'll run out of breastmilk."

"Pain can also be mortal and immortal. The pain that I have been dealt is immortal, do you understand? Immortal!" The memories stung her insides like splinters from a wet log, her head was pounding… She swallowed the tears that were filling her mouth… They were slightly salty, like blood. "I'll die, I can no longer bear it. I would rather die," Nakhshun wanted to collapse into his arms and cry her heart out, but she resisted.

"We have no say in this…" Harout was looking for the right words to console her, "We are simply messengers… carrier pigeons of sorts. You have to have something to bring with you if you want to be born, you have to have something to take away if you want to die. But you haven't even lived properly yet. If God has protected you so far…" Harout was unable to overcome his emotions, as if not wanting to speak in defense of the Lord, knowing deep in his soul that Nakhshun had been dealt the cruelest of deaths… He looked at the tears streaming down the woman's face and recalled the wooden, blank stare that he had seen in her eyes when she had appeared at the lake that first day. This caused his joy—"Life has returned to her," he thought, "Her pain now trusts the tears, and the tears trust the world into which they flow."

His knee was in great pain, it was killing him. Especially at night, in the surrounding peace, the pain would howl up to his heart like a coyote's call. The pain would ruin his sleep and he would sit under the pear tree and look at the world around him—in front of him lay what used to be Perch's house, which had been given to some of the migrants. Onés would also sometimes step outside, tortured by insomnia, and he would smirk when he saw Harout.

"How come you aren't sleeping?"

"My leg… the damn thing is killing me. It's no wonder they say that your soul ends up where your body hurts."

"So given that I have a hemorrhoid," Onés would ask, "Where is *my* soul?"

On one of those nights when there was nothing—no Onés, no howling dogs, no swooshing falcons—Nakhshun's door had suddenly opened and she had stepped outside. Harout had grown angry in his mind. "You've just given birth, where do you think you're going? You shouldn't be out in the moon's rays…" But then he seemed to realize that it was nighttime and that everyone was supposed to be asleep. Nakhshun would have nowhere to go at that hour and so, his heart full of suspicion, he dragged his hurting foot behind him as he followed her. Nakhshun knew the village well and walked carefully, walking through the yards and streets where there were no dogs. She would stop sometimes, placing her hand on her heart to catch her breath with her hand, glancing behind her to check… She left the village. "She must be missing… that animal!" Harout grew angry. He felt against the side of his waist. His knife was there. He would kill him. No doubt.

Like a child that creates a set of intermittent sounds "Ah, ah, ah…" by clapping his hand against his mouth in a rhythm, the wind that brought Sargis' moaning to his ears kept cutting it into a series of short sounds. He suddenly realized that the call was coming from another side, not the direction in which they were heading. That made him happy. But Nakhshun was nevertheless walking towards the mountains. "Is she going to throw herself off a cliff? If she's lived through the massacres and not taken her own life, why would she do so now?" Harout tried to calm himself. Nakhshun stopped a short distance after the wheat fields and turned around to see if anybody was there. She leaned against a rock and had a hand on her chest to catch her breath. After she had rested a bit, she removed her headdress and tied it around her face, the one would treat a broken jaw to immobilize it. Then she bent down and started to dig. She kept digging for a long time, and did so in rapid movements while stopping to look at the moon. She sneezed on several occasions from the dust that had filled her lungs and looked around in fear each time, thinking that everyone must have heard her. She dug a hole and examined its edges, unhappy about something. Then she slightly extended it on the left side and jumped into it, lying down at its bottom. She crossed her hands against her chest and closed her eyes. She remained there like that for a while. "Is she dead?" Harout was terrified. At this thought, Nakhshun sat up in the hole and dragged some of the soil onto her legs, then lay down again. She uncrossed her hands and placed them at her sides, then said the Lord's Prayer out loud. She emerged from the hole. She used her hands and legs to replace the soil back into the hole. She formed a mound, like one would do for a grave. She walked around this mound again—she was probably trying to determine which side would hold the head and which the feet. She made up her mind about this. She took out a small wooden cross from her pocket and stuck it into the upper corner of the mound with these words burned onto it using coal—My mother, Nunik. She took out some kindling wood from her broad skirt and placed it in front of the cross. She used one hand to protect the wood from the wind, and lit it with the other. When the fire had died out, she placed pinches of incense on its smoldering remains. "This one is from me... this is on my sister's behalf... this is my brother's... this is my father's..." She shook the piece of paper that held the incense and then dropped the paper into the fire. She drew a deep breath, then began to cry out loud, "This is for Aunt Anush... sister-in-law Vardik... Aghas... Uncle Vaghinak..." she kept mentioning names between these sobs for whom no pinches of incense remained. She held her head as she cried for half an hour. Then she suddenly stood up. She sniffed hard and wiped her eyes with the edge of her shawl. She returned.

The following two days, Harout's leg felt better. He had found some bear fat and that had helped tremendously. On the fourth day, he ran out of the fat and found himself sitting in his yard again, moaning as he placed his leg in a raised position on the tree that had been struck by lightning. And once again, Nakhshun's door opened. Nakhshun stepped outside. The times after that when he saw Nakhshun leaving her house at night, his leg hurt too much to follow her, but he knew where she was going. But he felt sorry for her, "So young and yet she buries herself every day. What a cruel fate to face..."

The twins were three years old when, one day, there was a storm. It was insignificantly brief and stretched across the sky like a tense nerve ending unexpectedly, hissing at the end of the neighborhood, then vanished. The people heard the sound of the wind approaching and then saw the dust flying over the roof of Nakhshun's house the next moment... Nakhshun ran out into the yard to bring the children indoors and saw that Anahit was still eating her cup of curd—she had lost her spoon in the grass somewhere and had grabbed a snake instead, stuffing its face into the cup, then licking it before stuffing it into the cup again for another lick. The reptile seemed to know that it was dealing with an innocent child—it had held its breath and did not show any signs of life, waiting patiently. At Nakhshun's screams, her neighbor Nektar ran out, rubbing her hands wet with them on her belly before noticing with terror how the child sitting in the grass was licking the curd off a snake's face happily, as if she were enjoying a lollipop. "She's a Turk, after all, a Turk!" she thought, shuddering with fear, "Even a snake would submit to one." But then she tried to calm Nakhshun down.

"Don't worry, snakes are wise creatures, it won't attack a child."

Nakhshun picked the child up, grabbed the curd-covered snake from her hand and threw it aside.

"It's not the snake that frightens me... Where's Astghik? Astghik was with her, the two of them were together... Where did she go? What happened?" Nakhshun was running this way and that in confusion, unsure of what to do, the child stuck to her bosom.

"I wonder if she loves her children," the neighbor thought to herself and went back in to wake up her husband who had stayed up most of the night at the *tonir* and, exhausted, ended up falling asleep at its side. "Hurry up," she ordered her complaining husband, "Vagho, run over to Harout's, the wind has carried away one of the twins..."

Vaghinak was wearing only one of his shoes and put the other on while running out the house; in his sleep-addled mind, he was rushing through the fields on the back of the Wild Horse... He ran over to ask Harout for his Wild Horse, which Harout—as those who recall the story still recount with laughter—had picked up one winter's day when he had left the village on foot but returned on horseback. He had stuffed Sato, and all of her hands and feet, into a sack made of salted buffalo skin and taken her with him. He had returned at dawn on horseback, alone—he had exchanged Sato for the steed.

"Are the diseased in our village condemned to die from now on?" the villagers had complained.

"Don't be afraid, I've loaned her for a week. There was a child in one of the villages on the lowlands that was dying of mumps, I felt sorry for them."

"Well, well…" Sahak had whistled after examining the horse, "Is Sato really worth this much?"

Harout laughed and did not tell him that he was supposed to additionally give a couple of lambs.

When Vaghinak rushed into his yard, Harout was saddling the horse.

"Brother," he hurried, catching his breath, "Quick, give me your horse…"

"What's wrong?" Harout laughed at the man's anxiety and the request he had just made.

"Brother, it came from the north side, twisted around the top of the mountain and rushed into the valley…"

"Vagho, what's wrong?" Harout repeated his question.

"That's what I'm trying to tell you. It came from the north side, twisted around the top of the mountain and rushed into the valley… If it came across an animal in the valley, it would have strangled it for sure… It picked up dust from the valley and turned its lazy eye at our village…"

"Vagho," Harout was running out of patience.

Vagho swallowed his spit in fear, looked at the horse's brushed mane and started again, trying to be convincing.

"Listen to me, brother. So, when it came from the north side, twisted around the top of the mountain and rushed into the valley… and then it picked up dust from the valley, I can't really be sure if it looked at our village with its lazy eye or the other one… it rushed over our village carrying dust and brushing against our rocks and bushes with its belly, opening up a path for itself as it entered the square, and then inhaled powerfully…"

Harout turned around angrily and continued fastening the saddle, no longer listening to him, bending down to the horse's belly to check whether the buckle was tight.

"Nakhshun has lost one of her twins," Vagho finally left the storm in peace and talked straight, offended by Harout's attitude to his story.

"What? Which one?" Harout exclaimed anxiously.

"The one that steals eggs from bird nests and eats them… It took her away, the wind… Right from their yard, she was with her sister and then vanished… Give me the horse, I'm telling you, I'll go check in the valley, you gather the villagers, give them orders… I hope nobody's killed her."

Harout looked at him in terror.

"Why would anyone kill an innocent person? A child, at that…" he asked without turning around, his hands still touching the horse's back, as if afraid that turning around and looking him in the eyes would infect him with the same fear and doubts.

"I don't know," Vagho muttered in a way that suggested he did know, "We're talking about a Turk here, not a child."

Harout froze for a second, then grabbed him by the collar and picked him up off the ground, shouting,

"Those are Nakhshun's children, and Nakhshun is an Armenian. An Armenian! An Armenian!"

"Harout *jan*," Vagho mumbled, not knowing what to say, "I didn't mean it like that… I meant that the villagers may have looked at it that way."

"Vagho!" he heard Nektar's voice at that moment, "She's been found."

The woman appeared in the distance, the child in her arms, chewing tree gum. Harout let go of Vagho's collar.

"Damn you to hell…" Vaghinak exhaled with relief as he looked towards the child, "Were you playing a game with us? Where was she?" he shouted his questions.

"She'd crawled into the doghouse and fallen asleep there," the woman, now closer, said.

"That one strangles snakes, this one crawls into doghouses… The poor animals are suffering a lot at their hands!" Vagho joked, "Keep them away from these kids."

Nektar came closer.

"Because of this naughty thing…" she shook the child playfully and bit her soft cheek, "Nakhshun went to hell and back… and took us with her!"

The child she was carrying held out her hands in Harout's direction. He picked up the smiling, mischievous girl from the woman and asked, "Where were you, you naughty thing? Had the wind carried you away? Were you lost?" He tapped the child's nose playfully and scolded Nakhshun in his mind, "Why did you have to be so honest? You could have lied and said that the Turks had killed your husband after you were pregnant with his children… Millions of Armenians were slaughtered and orphans, who would have wanted to check the lineage of your children?" He had seen women in Etchmiadzin with watery wounds on their breasts and cheeks… Pretty girls had rubbed stones and sand against their faces, cutting themselves, trying to feign leprosy so that nobody would touch them… But Nakhshun had not displayed even that simple cunning and was now suffering because of her naiveté. "Stupid woman, her honesty will make these children's lives more difficult." He bounced the child in his arms but could not forget the terror in Vagho's voice when he had suggested getting the villagers together. He decided at that moment that he would start doing rounds twice or thrice a day, both before and after dark, to peek into their house and make sure nobody was bothering them. "That's what love is…" That was how the women of the village interpreted this as they made their way to collect water.

Nakhshun was sitting on a tuffet, her knitting at her knees, but her gaze sometimes slipping away from her task to cast a quick look at the girls whispering to each other under the sheet, feigning terror as she said, "Oh dear, what a powerful storm! Go to sleep, or it will carry you away!" The girls would laugh at their mother's fear. They knew that everything was a bit exaggerated in these parts, just like the mountains were nothing but exaggerated rocks, coming down from so high up that they might as well be the roots of the sky, feeling for the air around them as they descended and finally came to rest on the ground. What they called a storm in these parts was just a strong wind, and they referred to their lake as the sea,
"Oh dear…" they said, mimicking their mother.
Nakhshun poked at the pattern with her needle, used a threader to insert the colorful yarn, and continued to knit. The yarn was a ball at first, then grew into a leaf and a flower… Fatigued, she stabbed a finger and the blood brushed against the white material, "Oh no…" Nakhshun was upset at what she had done.
"No need to be upset," Anahit said, consoling her mother, "Nobody's going to buy that from you anyway."
"Hmph," Astghik grunted, "Do they think they can find anything prettier?"
"They say that a newlyweds' bedding must be made by a woman that has a husband… Misfortune, they say, can be passed on…"
"Go to sleep!" Nakhshun shouted at the girls, dropping the knitting angrily on the tuffet and stepping out.
There was a strong wind, and a red tail of lighting wagged over the distant mountains. The clouds that were challenging the peaks would burst

with searing, icy drops of rain if they advanced one more step. She made up her mind. Since it had not yet started to rain, since the wind that was twisting itself up inside her and rattling the rocks in her belly, crashing all the sounds in the world together and smashing into rooftops, this was the right time—she would go to Harout again. She had not forgotten the gossip, of course, but they posed no obstacle and they certainly were no longer news. They had always been there, especially when she went to Harout before he set off for the broader world and talked with him for hours about her relatives, friends, and neighbors, describing them in detail so that Harout would immediately recognize them if he saw them anywhere. When he returned, she would be the first person to see him as she walked up to meet him halfway, hoping to get a piece of news. "Anybody else would have lost their minds at this point in their life, but this one is playing love games," the women of the village had no sympathy for Nakhshun.

"She isn't like them, that's why they treat her that way..." Sato would explain, "Put a chick into a flock of ducklings and see what happens. They'll peck it to death. Also... she's completely closed herself off, she doesn't talk to anyone. She doesn't go to visit anyone, nor does she host the others. That woman has concealed herself from God, she never leaves her house. Good Lord, doesn't she get bored? Doesn't she miss the sunlight?" She astonished Harout too.

"Fine," he would think, "She sews, she knits, so she has work to do—but *that* much?" So he decided to check. He slipped in unnoticed one day and saw her bent over her knitting again. He was angry. "Take it easy on yourself," he said, "You'll ruin your eyes, don't do this anymore. I'll give you all the money you need."

"It's not for the money," Nakhshun explained, "I have set myself an objective." Harout looked at her lap—a beautiful white dress with a wavy skirt, a small bird and flower embroidered on it, the cloud and sky as yet unfinished, the string still hanging on the needle. He did not know what to say.

"It's pretty," he muttered.

"I like it too," Nakhshun said with pride, and then opened up. "I can't hide this from you, like I can't hide it from God... I never had a wedding veil or a white dress, but... I'm going to dance. I'm going to dance when my girls get married, I'll be done with this dress by that time. I'll put it on and dance. I don't care what anyone says. I'm going to dance!"

Nakhshun felt that Harout knew everything about her anyway, he was her only supporter and protector, there was no point in hiding anything from him, especially since she would not be able to do what she had planned without him.

The wind slithered up the spine of the mountains in the bright darkness of the autumn night, scratching the sky with a strangled scream, hanging itself from the ragged clouds and slipping down, praying sounds and dust from the place where it fell, pressing the rocks to the ground clawing at rocks and bushes with nail-less fingers, grabbing its own tail in its mouth as it rolled about wildly, thrashing and slithering… and whizzing… Like being skinned alive, the wind was ripping itself apart.

Protecting herself against the bone-piercing wind, Nakhshun placed her hands on her chest to stop it from penetrating and taking everything she had inside; she used a foot to kick the gate open.

Harout stopped at the door. He used one hand to protect his hair and the other to cover his waist from the wind. He hesitated and remained standing there for a while. The blurred light of the lamp flickered through a crack in the wooden door. Should he knock, or enter without knocking?

"What have you decided?" Harout was startled at the sudden sound of her voice.

"You give me no peace. What would people think, seeing you like this… in the middle of the night, wearing just one layer of clothing," Harout looked at her delicate, sleek body, the shoulders that had been folded into her arms due to the cold and her fear, the transparent skin of her hands, through which her green veins shimmered, and thought, "It's a lie that we are born naked… We are born wearing our own skin like a set of clothing."

"I've put aside some money, it should be enough…" Sorrow flowed from Nakhshun's eyes.

"Don't make me laugh…" Harout had only now understood why Nakhshun would always bring him some of her handmade items to sell whenever he travelled for trade.

"Please ask for gold in return, if you can…" she muttered, as if to justify what she said, "I've set myself an objective."

Harout did not tell her that things were terrible in the outside world – with so much death, hunger and blood out there, who would think about buying lace? He would gift her items to the people he knew and give Nakhshun some of the money he got from selling fish, pretending that it was what he had been given for her items. He thought she was putting the money aside for her daughters' dowry. He felt even more sorry for her, thinking that she had given up on living and deprived herself of life, simply to waste her existence on such things. He thought for a moment that if he had managed to save his mother, she would have been the same way.

"What difference does it make to you? We'll do it in secret. I can come with you, if you want. We'll be done in a couple of days and we'll return," Nakhshun said stubbornly, "You'll tell everyone that we're going out into the world for trade."

"That's all I needed... You and I... They're already gossiping about us all the time," as he spoke, Harout looked out the window at a dog—asleep with its head in its paws—to keep from betraying how he truly felt. Then he looked helplessly at Nakhshun thinking whether he should propose that they sit down, or would this be impolite. A thick sweetness of boiling aromas burned his throat from the inside...

Nakhshun stood there, unsmiling like Christ, careful to avoid letting life approach her a second time. "If the sky only knew what she had truly allowed to happen..." Harout thought achingly.

He walked up to Nakhshun and held her hand, rubbing her cold fingers in his palm for a moment—that same coldness would be on Nakhshun's back right now, and on her shoulders... but then he suddenly realized that Nakhshun might think this was how he wanted her to pay him back and, ashamed at that thought, he let her go, leaving the warmth of his hand on her cold fingers.

"Try to understand," he said, hesitating, "A village full of husbandless and lonely women are jealous of you, wearing you down..."

"If you reject me this time as well, I'll leave this village of yours. I'll take my children and I'll run away, I'll go out into the world."

Harout did not believe her.

"No time would be better," he smirked incredulously, "This is the season when the wolves are hungry."

Having passed through the man-eating deserts full of Turkish bandits, Nakhshun knew now that life was a battlefield where even God had been defeated and his Resurrection had been nothing but a beautifully presented escape. But, nevertheless, she had to make a last attempt—she had to win.

And she had fixated her teary and stubborn gaze on Harout as a person on death row who would look at the sky for the last time.

"I'll leave," she said, confidently.

When Harout had taken the oxen out of the stable, she said,

"I know that you are like family," Nakhshun stuffed the money into his palm and caressed the red ox's back tenderly, "Give them whatever they ask for, don't think too much about it being too expensive or too cheap."

Walking behind the oxen, Harout realized just then why the village women did not like Nakhshun. They had different reasons to live, they had nothing in common. Nakhshun did not realize that life is a good thing and that one could gain pleasure from living. In her imagination, life was a series of deprivations and humiliations, from which one had to emerge with as much dignity as possible. Perhaps this had been dictated by the reputation of her wealthy father? Perhaps she would go in a carriage to the churchyard and step outside without looking around, then go inside, sing with her eyes fixated to the image of the Holy Virgin, and return home. It's hard to imagine her running free in the mountains and valleys in her youth, the sounds of her own laughter drowning each other out, as Sato's girl had once done, though she was now hidden beneath the rock salt as he took her to give her to her father because the man had become an invalid, and the girl could now cook food... And she had learned a few things from Harout. Recalling Sato's daughter, Harout laughed contentedly to himself. And he laughed well, without holding anything back.

The mountain hung above him. The clouds hung above the mountains. The sky hung above the clouds, and above that hung the sun... What hung above the sun? Only God knew. God's shadow fell upon the sun, the sun's shadow fell upon the clouds, the clouds' shadow upon the mountains, and there he stood with his oxen, in the shadow of the mountains. And the oxen were mighty, pulling the cart along... The wheels of the cart dug into the ground under its weight, pushing out the sinewy soil as the mountain slope croaked beneath them.

"Hey, we're almost there, not much left," Harout consoled his oxen and scolded Perch in his mind as he stared into the blurry distance. "There's no need to isolate yourself in the mountains if you want to hide, it's easier to hide among people. On the other hand, it makes no difference whether you're hiding in the mountains, among people, or inside yourself. What matters is that, when you die, you can give back to God in its purest form the things that you received from Him in purity."

Like a stubborn disease, the road was torturous. When it twisted, Harout twisted with it, when it sloped downwards, Harout went downhill on his oxen, when it went uphill, Harout whipped his oxen to keep them moving upward… Whatever the road ordered him to do, he obeyed, but it was not going to be enough. The wheels of the cart screeched with the rocks they hit, the thirsty oxen gradually put their feet more slowly into the grainy clay soil and kept them there longer, the rocks cracked in the dominating dryness. The wind was suffocating, grabbing away the last bit of air right after bringing it to his face. The dry twigs of red sorrel were bending in the wind, spraying overripe pollen on the thick heads of the oxen, but the beasts did not flinch and kept moving. Although Harout held out a hand to grab hold of the cart a couple of times and keep it from rolling downwards, he was not scared and did not stop. Hurricanes and strong winds were common things in these parts.

His heels were moaning and he thought of sitting in the cart, but he felt sorry for the oxen. "These poor creatures are going to need a month to recover from this. But what can I do?" He swallowed with emotion, "I could not bear that woman's tears, I could not reject her. But I should have. In these times of hunger… But she works hard, pricking her nails with needles, bending her body in half. It's a waste of her money, but what can I say? Everyone has their own calculations when it comes to life," he moaned, using a hand to protect his face from sorrel seeds, "But I wouldn't do that." He stopped for a moment and looked back—was anyone following him, had anyone seen him leave? The mountain was behind him, pretending to be a hand placed below the sky's chin—if it were to slip, the sky would flow down and swallow the world. The road wound ahead of him, seemingly cut into bits like a bunch of stuttering words as it rose to the sky, up to the swollen clouds that were arched above him in plump bulges. He had also looked down from the top of the mountain; it was like a recently departed soul looking down at its body. He looked down at the world, coddling it within him—all its ruins, refugees, wars and revolutions—and then turned away with relief and continued his path.

The green mountains blended with the darkness and first turned blue, then black, finally dissolving into obscurity. The oxen were tired but kept pushing their hooves hard into the ground and slowly moving their load. A myriad sound rang out in the mountains, coming down to mix with the exhaled breath of the exhausted creatures. Who was talking to whom in those dull murmurs of the night, the barking and howling, the snorting and hissing… What was flowing in the veins of the universe that caused such sounds to come from its depths?

Harout was not afraid. He knew that the sun would return soon, just like a criminal always returns to the scene of the crime. When he entered the village, the moon was still a blurred memory in the milky darkness, but an immature sun was already pushing its thorns out of the other end of the sky.

Hrayr the cow herder, his meal for the day stuffed into a small bag he held in his hand, appeared in his path.

"Harout? You'd gone out into the world? What's new?"

"Nothing's new," Harout sighed, "The orphans cry differently now, the saints have changed their prayers, but everything in the world is the same."

"What have you brought with you this time?" Hrayr examined the straw-covered cart.

"Nothing, brother," he looked at the barely moving cart, "What power do we humans have to do anything? What can we bring with us? Nothing."

"I see," Hrayr extended the word and smiled mysteriously, then he ran up to the approaching cows.

Harout did not go home. He turned the oxen's head towards the Torn Mountain. Nakhshun was waiting for him there, her shawl tightly wound around her narrow waist, uneasy with emotion but so excited that she was unable to feel the thorny chill of dawn. At the very spot where she would come at night to dig a hole and bury herself, then get up and light incense… That was where he dropped the load. The cross-stone slid off the cart and thumped onto the ground.

"It's not straight," Nakhshun tried to push and adjust it, her hands pressing against the stone, but she moaned weakly.

"It's impossible to move," Harout examined his cargo in the light of day. "It has the weight of a mountain; how could somebody move it?"

Like that night so many years ago, Nakhshun took out some incense and matches as well as some kindling wood from her skirt and lit it, dropping the incense into the fire and… Harout bore witness to the grandeur that comes only with a mourning ceremony in the east—songs, tears, promises, requests, expressions of love, hope and despair…

"If only there were a priest who could bless it," tired of mourning, Nakhshun wiped her nose.

"Why would someone bless a grave?" Harout was upset, "One should bless the living."

"It needs to be blessed… God's blessings are needed in any situation in life.

"What for?" Harout stared at the gravestone skeptically, not wanting to add, "How can you bless something that isn't there?"

Nakhshun seemed to catch the unspoken words.

"I mean, who am I to criticize God's ways? But that's not right, it's just not right…"

"God is not to blame that the humans have come up with truths that do not match His."

Nakhshun took a deep breath.

"Why doesn't it have the name and dates of birth and death on it?"

"I don't know. You hadn't told me which of your family members this was for. That's why I had them inscribe, 'I…' Indefinite, but clear. What matters is that everyone will understand that someone has been laid to rest." He was irritated at Nakhshun's care for that piece of stone as she caressed it and walked around it, examined its corners, the inscribed patterns. She was rubbing the cross and kissing it from time to time. "I don't understand why you needed this."

"My children must have roots and a foundation…" Nakhshun said and went silent with satisfaction, continuing to caress the cross. Then she added, "Until a priest has said a prayer here, this will not become a grave." And she was lost in thought until she suddenly recalled something and exclaimed, "I know where we can find a priest!"

"Where can we find a priest?" Harout was surprised. He even found the thought funny—find a priest in those years of socialism, when priests were being hunted in groups, just like he caught schools of fish, and churches were being burned? But one could forgive Nakhshun for that—after all, Harout didn't tell the people of his village these things. He would leave the misfortune of the outside world at the foot of the hill, like a tired farmer leaves his dusty boots at the threshold of the door before coming in.

"Yes—Haiké!" Nakhshun looked cunningly at Harout and said this with excitement, then fell quiet with regret. And she recalled her grandmother, who would put aside money and keep this a secret from her husband, then justify her actions with a laugh and say, "You should show one cheek of your behind to your man, but not the other." They weren't man and wife, but nonetheless... Haiké was the perfect choice. He was the son of the priest at the same monastery where she used to sing. The Turks had stormed the monastery and killed everyone, slaughtering the priest and forcing his son to drink his blood. He had lost his mind then and there.

"Haiké?" Harout turned in surprise so that Nakhshun would not see his eyes mock her, "But he's crazy!"

"He isn't crazy, he's the heir of a priest."

"So what? We're the heirs of God, but we're not God... You can see how far we are from being God," he used his head to indicate the cross-stone weighing into the ground. "To this day, he has acted like he's crazy, and everyone has treated him like he's crazy."

Before Harout's eyes, the scene replayed when the nets had got tangled and enmeshed in something at the bottom of the lake. He had been forced to spend the night at the lake, but the cold wind had struck against his lungs and he was boiling with fever, his swollen throat was suffocating him. Even vodka did not help, the constriction got worse. He had some white spirit, which he had received in exchange for dried fish somewhere near Erivan. He remembered that he had placed it at the bottom of his grain silo. He used a skewer to poke around and removed some rags, wrapped around a one-liter bottle of white spirit. He opened it and took a sip. He raised his chin and let it slide down his throat. He gargled and then spat it out, closing the bottle. The insides of his eyes were warm and burning. He stepped outside with the bottle of white spirit in his hands. Sato wrapped a piece of cloth around her finger, dipped that into the white spirit and cleaned Harout's throat.

"Spit," she said as she removed her finger, "It smells terrible in there, there's pus in your throat."

Harout's eyes had teared up and he caught his breath and spat.

"It's hard, it's not coming loose," Sato dipped her finger in the spirit again and stuck in inside Harout's mouth, "Your throat is really swollen. But don't worry, I'll increase the swelling to make it explode, so that the pus can flow out."

She grabbed the edges of her shawl and folded them, turning it into a thick rope. She made Harout kneel on the floor and stood before him, flinging the rope across his neck. "Don't move your head, stay in the same position," and she moved the rope across his neck one way, then the other. "Swelling, swelling," she said in a melodious voice, pulling it upwards in a fast motion on several occasions. Harout moaned.

"Hang in there, not much left. One more time."

She moved the shawl rope against his neck again and pulled it up rapidly, as if wanting to lift him off the ground.

"Spit out now! Did it work?" She turned around and examined the contents of his sputum in the uneven plate. "Have someone come over to your place tonight. If the pus doesn't flow out, you're going to suffer a bit. There's the risk that you'll lose consciousness… Don't stay alone! Or go down to the inner district and ask Jano to blow in your mouth. That'll take care of it in an instant."

Harout returned with Sato's shawl wrapped around his neck. Arsho, Sogho's wife, was waiting near the door, a floury sack at her feet.

"I've brought it back, brother… Don't think for a moment that I don't want to be part of this… I'm human too, I want to help out… But this guy's crazy!" She kicked the sack lightly with her foot, "Take this one and give me another corpse. Please understand me—he's crazy, and we're only human." She bent over and unfastened the mouth of the sack, then turned it over and dumped its contents—Haiké.

The young man stretched slightly on the soil, wriggled like a worm, then began to stare at the sky and froze.

"What has he been doing?"

"He laughs for no apparent reason."

"So what?"

"Come on, so what? If it starts with unexpected laughter, can you imagine how it'll end? I have three daughters, as you know, and this young man is reaching maturity, and he sees them, he laughs…. Anything is possible, it's too risky, I'm sorry…" her words flooded out and she turned away without looking at Harout, and left.

"I don't know… I mean, all he does is laugh to himself," Harout laid down his resistance at the sight of Nakhshun's reprimanding eyes.

"And if that is all we get from him... it would still be good enough," Nakhshun sighed.

Without losing any time, Nakhshun went the following day to the house that Harout had built for Haiké. After Sogho's wife Arsho had carried him over and emptied the sack of him at Harout's feet, he had lived for a brief time at Harout's, but Harout liked his solitude as much as he did his freedom. So he built him a house. He told the women that cared for his animals to feed him and wash his clothes. Harout had later given in on his preferred way of life too, because Nakhshun had come and quietly settled into his solitude, like a prayer on a pair of sinful lips, like gold in the darkness of a safe.

When she got there, Nakhshun saw that the young cowherders were pushing him around, beating him as they dragged him toward the village. It turned out that Haiké had been digging around in the playground and had found something shiny and round.

"Gold, gold," the children were shouting gleefully, jumping around and dancing, "We've found gold..."

In all this merriment, Haiké had taken the piece of gold and thrown it away.

"Why did you do that, man? Didn't you see that it was gold? Didn't you see your friends getting happy about it?"

"I did see," Haiké shuddered, "And I thought it would be good if someone else found it and felt the same joy..."

Nakhshun snatched him from among the boys and took him with her.

"I'll say the prayer, you make the sign of the cross, like your father..."

The children playing the "evil spirits" of the Feast of the Ascension first plucked out handfuls of the yellow leaves of the Flower of Good Fortune, sucked its nectar out and threw it away. When they had had their fill, they wove wreaths made of flowers and evergreen branches, put them on the girls' heads, and walked down to the village. Flour sieves hung from their waists and the girls walked in front, with the young boys coming up from behind, everyone singing, "Praise be to, praise be to... who should we praise? Praise be to Grandma Haykush!" And Grandma Haykush shuffled into the corners of the house, picking up eggs and sweets, which she placed into the sieves of the "evil spirits" so that they would keep misfortune away from her home for the year, in exchange. Satisfied with their haul from this house, the children covered in flowers and grass moved on to the next one. "Praise be to, praise be to… who should we praise?" Sweets, dried fruits, eggs, bread, cheese, *halva*… Their sieves almost full, the children turned towards the Turks' district. "Praise be to, praise be to…" but the song was suddenly interrupted and little Harout's hoarse voice rang out, "Harout! They're beating Nakhshun!" When Harout rushed over, some people had already separated the ones who were fighting. Nakhshun was slowly getting up from the ground and dusting off her skirt, Bero still muttered to herself, chewing on her anger. Harout had unfastened the horsehair rope from his waist, and was using the hooked pieces of iron at its ends to whip the ground beneath him as he waited for answers.

"His son called us a Turk… He deserved the beating he got," Astghik explained.

"Well, you're Turks, aren't you?" Bero went on the offensive, "That's exactly what you are, murderers… You almost plucked my child's eye out." She turned her son towards Harout so that he could see his swollen, bloodshot eye. Harout was still waiting for Bero to explain, and he spanked the rocks at her feet with the iron hooks on the horsehair rope.

"I have no regrets," said Bero, who had not been with a man for more than 20 years and who took the whipping of the horsehair rope against the rocks as an expression of Harout's love for Nakhshun. "Take a look at the long shape of their heads… That's exactly what Turks' heads look like. Why did these people come and divide our wholesome village into Armenians and Turks?"

"Don't ever say that word again!" Harout shouted curtly, as if curling his words into a fist that would strike Bero.

"You heartless thing," Bero was livid as she snapped at Nakhshun, "Why didn't you jump off a cliff, like so many others did, instead of giving yourself to those Turks and then bringing these creatures into our fold?"

"Suicide?" Noyemi was among the gathering and was offended. "How could you justify yourself before God after that? It is better to be humiliated before humankind than before God."

"Oh, come on…" Bero spat our condescendingly, "If she had any value before God, these things wouldn't have happened to her."

Harout lifted his murky gaze off Bero as if he were moving a huge weight. He hung his head and walked away, continuing to whip the ground beneath him as he left. A short while later, the cart and oxen were at Bero's door.

"Harout *jan*, be reasonable. What did I do? I was just protecting my child," Bero was weeping, "If only my jaw had broken and I had not spoken those words... Where will you take my fatherless children and me? How can we live anywhere else?"

"Bero, we even deny God when he takes things too far... You've gone too far as well. If you're really thinking about the wellbeing of your father-less children," Harout spoke calmly but continued to strike the ground with his rope, "You should hurry up so that we aren't forced to leave after dark."

Bero's elder daughter walked up and threw her sieve full of sweets in the dust at Harout's feet, stared at him with wrath and then walked back in. She came out with a bedsheet, which she placed in Harout's cart and then stared at him threateningly before going back indoors.

Harout returned ten days later. They said he had taken them to the area around Aran, where Bero's family had to settle into a new home. Her small-bodied children were neither able to go fishing in these parts, nor could they work as laborers in the city there. But the soil in Aran was good, it would bear two harvests a year. And Bero's children were hard working—they would till the land and grow crops. And they said that it took exactly ten days to go to Aran and return.

On the day he returned, Sato came to see him. Had he managed to bring the honeybee royal jelly and white spirit she had requested? As she babbled about this and that, she slipped in something else in a matter-of-fact way,

"Nakhshun's completely lost her mind after that damned fight... It's like she can't think straight anymore, you should go see her..." she said and left, without any emotion or additional explanation. Harout asked no questions. When it was dark—although he had always avoided showing up not just in their house, but even in their yard, given that she was raising two young girls and neither they nor their neighbors were used to a man's presence—he went to visit Nakhshun. Nakhshun was sitting there, her knitting in her lap, her head bent over as always, her needle in the middle of making a pattern. She leaped up with surprise when she saw him, dropping the knitting to the floor and swaying as she tried to keep on her feet.

"I feel dizzy... from the crying and the beating," she explained.

Harout looked her over, trying to find something unusual in what she said or how she behaved.

"I've thought of something smart," Nakhshun said, without looking him in the eyes. Harout said down beside her, looking at the children asleep on the rug, and asked in a whisper,

"And?"

"Take me away from here, drop me off in the outside world… I can't take it anymore, what kind of a life is this? The people in your village are savages, they don't care for God or prayer."

"They do," Harout consoled her, "But they don't make much use of them, because it never ended up saving them… as it was with you."

"Well, I can't keep living without prayer… So what should we do? Take me away from here!"

"Where?" He was sure that nobody would be able to answer this question he had asked, so he tried to persuade her, "Believe me when I say there is nowhere better for you… If the issue here is only with God and prayer, then the outside world doesn't care for humans and humanity. People don't pray out there, they beat their prayers with tears the way one beats one's chest in mourning… The world is a desert, Nakhshun, a desert of human solitude…"

"Help me," she slipped to the ground and fell at Harout's feet, "I need to baptize my children… You have to get them baptized, we have to get that ugly name washed off my children with holy chrism."

"Is this a joke?"

"Help my orphans…"

Harout stood up.

"Fine," he snapped laconically, and left.

"Anahit? Astgh? Ano?" the children of the neighborhood kept calling out.

"What's up, kids?" Nakhshun stood in her doorway.

"Can they come out and play?"

"They can't. They're not well."

"Oh no! My grandma made some soup. Do you want me to go and bring some?"

"No, no, no…" Nakhshun was startled, "They have chicken pox, you'll all catch it!" And she rushed back into the house.

It rained that evening. The sky seemed so close that the thunder rumbled in one's ear. Nakhshun was hurrying here and there in fear. She closed the stable door, then covered the straw… In her mind, she went over what she had done, recalling things in sequence once again. They had taken a sleeping potion from Sato, given it to the girls, hid them under the rock salt, and Harout had left at night and taken them to be baptized.

At dawn, after Nakhshun had dozed off and woken up several times, feeling each roar of thunder within her belly, the door suddenly creaked open. When she opened her eyes, Harout was already placing the sleeping Astghik in her bed, and he then stepped out to get Anahit. Nakhshun looked at them with joy.

"Glory to you, Lord," she whispered as she caressed Astghik's neck, removed the cross from the tricolor string, kissed it and crossed herself.

"Thank you so much..." her eyes teared over with joy as she took Harout by the hand after he had returned and carefully placed the sleeping Anahit in her bed. "Who was their godfather? When the children grow up, we'll go and find him. The world will probably be different then—it can't stay this way forever, can it? We'll build a relationship with our godfather. They're quite old now, my girls. They'll be able to remember his face, his name, his village."

"I don't think so..." Harout mumbled.

"What do you mean? Didn't you get them baptized?" There was a mixture of hate and terror in Nakhshun's eyes.

"I got them baptized... sniff their foreheads—can't you smell the chrism? It's just that the children have not woken up since that day... they never knew they were being baptized... it's better that way."

Harout got up. He turned around when he was in the doorway.

"Don't be scared. They'll wake up in the morning. I should leave while it's still dark, I don't want any more gossip going around," he smiled at Nakhshun, who was glowing with joy, and left.

"Yes, go get some sleep, you poor thing," Nakhshun said, "Go sleep, get some rest."

Harout closed the door behind him and took a deep breath of the cold, dense, milky air, then hurried his steps. Then he recalled something and stopped suddenly.

Nakhshun was crouched next to her children and arose, startled, when Harout walked in. She looked at him expectantly.

"I forgot," Harout said sheepishly, his hand going to his breast pocket, "I've brought you a gift," and he took something out, wrapped in a flowery cloth for children, which he held out to her. Nakhshun took it and carefully unwrapped the present.

"It's Narek's *Book of Lamentations*!"[6] she screamed with awe.

Harout said a silent thanks to the disguised salesman from whom he had bought guns on several occasions—he knew the person could be trusted to remain quiet. He had asked him to get him a Bible, but the man had probably been afraid of trouble, so he had given this instead. "It's a book that's equal to the Bible," he had said, refusing to accept any payment, "You cannot compare these words to any money… Take it, you deserve it."

"Do you like it?" he asked, although the answer was already obvious. "What is it about? They say it's a book that's equal to the Bible."

"It's Narek's book," Nakhshun's white fingers raised the book to her mouth and she kissed it before putting it aside, "He talks to God, face to face."

"He knows God?" Harout could not believe it.

"He does," Nakhshun confirmed, her eyes moving warmly from the book to Harout.

"How terrible…" Harout thought to himself, "Knowing something limits its freedom. God would not like that."

"All right," he got up and looked towards the sleeping girls. "I'm off."

When the door closed and Nakhshun, looking out the window, was convinced that Harout was gone, she wrapped the book in the flowery cloth again, pressed it to her chest, stayed that way for a moment, then put it on the wooden table, where the candle would sometimes crackle and flicker.

She knelt next to her sleeping children's beds. She felt for their crosses and removed them once again from under their clothing. She unfastened the tricolor strings from which they hung and placed the crosses on the bed, caressing them. "Hold on tight to these," she talked to her girls in her thoughts, "These are your souls, the only things you possess… These are the only things you've inherited from God, hold on tight to them." She wrapped the colorful string around each of the crosses and took them away for safe-keeping while her children slept. Then she glanced at the door, first in fear, before thinking warmly about Harout, "How many fates are entwined with

....

6   This is a reference to the *Book of Lamentations* by Gregory of Narek, an Armenian monk and poet that lived in the 10-11th century.

[74]

his in this village? How many times has that poor man come and gone in the night? How many tons of rock salt has he carried with those tired oxen of his…"

Thieves, sluts, hussies—the sisters could justifiably be called these things. But they were pretty.

"When a Turk is beautiful, nothing can be better," the villagers would say in awe.

"Why only a Turk? Kurds, Circassians, Lezgins… there are probably so many bloodlines involved here—how could you expect them to be ugly?" the women, tired of the sisters and the fights they started, said haughtily.

The immigrants were good artisans. They quickly pierced through the mountain, got under its skin, extracted clay and started to make *tonirs* and jugs. Nakhshun sewed bedsheets for newlyweds, little slippers for newborns, sheets with baklava-shaped, oval, or flowery patterns. "Here's to many warm nights together," she would say as she made that final stitch, as if she were restoring the dignity that the Turks' had robbed from her own bed. They even planted trees in the open gaps of those high mountains, providing cover from the wind and chill. But the sisters' behavior was enough to cancel out all these efforts.

The sisters worked with clay. They would go with the men to the mountains, bring back clay, carrying it to the village with them, where they would mix it with eggs, hay and water. They would knead the mixture with their bare feet and hike up the skirts that had grown heavy with wet clay, and the burning stares of the men looking at their bare legs would also be rubbed into the clay as they trampled on it. The jugs they made would be stuffed with wheat, baked cheese, cottage cheese, pickled radishes, thyme, and sorrel, which Harout would load onto his cart and cover with the dried skins of sheep, wolves, and foxes, before taking them from Bayazet to Erivan, and from them to Ararat and Artashat, where he would sell or barter them off. They would sell their ware in the village too—plates, cups, jugs and pitchers, toys… But woe be to anyone who would buy from one and not the other, or who would praise one's work in the other's presence. The sisters square up against each other and a fight would break out. One would say to the another, "What a waste of my mother's milk!" and the other would say, "What a waste of my mother's patience!" There wasn't a day when they wouldn't lash out at each other—their mother was still in this world, but they were already ruining her place in the next. In a village where one's mother's grave was worth more than the mother herself, the sisters' fighting caused a level of disgust akin to cannibalism.

"Damn the road that brought you here..." the villagers would curse.

Nakhshun would shrink and feel shame at her daughter's behavior, as well as that of the world... She would stick her nose in the armpit and cry silently.

The immigrant Onés would praise Nakhshun, trying to mollify the villagers' wrath.

"Do you know whose granddaughters they are? Do you know what kind of a man Nakhshun's father was? He would give the poor forty sheep to eat every day. Do you know what kind of a man her betrothed was? He would teach forty children a day how to read. Do you know who her brother was? And her, too! How she would sing! And what a great *knjru* she makes," his parade of praise would stretch on, "You've never tasted *knjru* like that before," and Onés would close his eyes dreamily.

There were also those that wished Nakhshun well. Asaneth even came to ask for a bride for her immature son.

"I'll agree to whichever of the two you give," she smiled to Nakhshun. She had also brought a handful of sugar, "Don't think too hard about it. When it comes to girls, their good fortune lies with the first person who asks for their hand. The ones that come later are no better."

Whenever she saw Asaneth's immature son—and the villagers would say that he would do all kinds of things with the animals up in the mountains—Nakhshun would always shudder and think, "Oh God... Nature can curse people with all kinds of afflictions."

"I don't see a man there," Nakhshun quietly responded, "So I can't consider this to be my daughter's good fortune."

"There's not much point in thinking too hard about it, sister. She'll bear a child and have an heir, she'll have a house to run. Look at my house, with its garden and livestock..."

"You can only appreciate a garden and livestock when you have a real man by your side," Nakhshun sighed, "And the man's seed must be of good quality... so that the offspring that comes from him does not end up being a burden... They say he is not all there."

"Well, so what?" Asaneth would not back down, "After all, you're Turks!" she spat out and left. But this had not been enough to calm her down. Outside, she had declared loud enough for the neighbors to hear, "You can keep your gluttonous girls to yourself... if someone is happy to put anything and everything here," she pinched three fingers together and raised them to her mouth, "The same would hold for down here too," and she had moved the pinched fingers to the area between her legs. "Let them keep it to themselves..."

After she had gone, Nakhshun remained seated for a long time, a frozen expression on her face, her arms folded into her lap, not allowing herself to shed a tear, staring curtly, roughly and angrily at the mountains that seemed to rise up endlessly. "It's too bad the world has to end here, in this way."

The three of them had to share the blame—the hens that were not laying any eggs, Sato, who had chosen to remind Nakhshun of her debt in the most public of places, and the river that was finding itself unable to absorb the screams coming from Nushik's house, such that the whole village knew that mother and son were killing each other there. And the wind too, which could blur out any sounds and lock them up in the caves, was bringing the whispers of the young people to the village, as if on purpose. In a word, nobody was surprised at the events that unfolded—they seemed to meet everyone's expectations of what was going to happen... Before that, when the villagers would complain to Nushik, saying, "Your son is going down to the gardens at night with Anahit, and they're damaging the potato crop there with their shenanigans – marry him off!" she would huff condescendingly, "I don't care how many of you say this... I'm not one to let her cross over my threshold." Then she realized that her son did not approve of her attitude towards the girl, and the neighbors counselled her as well, "Listen, woman," they said, "You can catch more flies with honey. What right do you have to judge her?" Nushik straightened and began to calmly lecture, "Someone born like that cannot be a normal person... The pain they've been through... It will resonate for centuries in their blood... Who can find happiness at their side? You will end up suffering for the rest of your life because of the destiny that was dealt to them." In the end, the river began to gargle up their quarrels, as it spat up their curses and bounced them from one of its banks to the other.

When the news came, Harout was chopping the tree that had been struck by lightning. And that was exactly how he ran down to the Dry Valley—the ax still in his hand. Little Harout had been beaten up, the blood was gushing from his nose and pouring into his mouth. The boy was suffocating, vomiting, but the blood kept flowing faster than he managed to spit it out. He was feeling the taste of blood for the first time and kept calling out to his friends in panic, "Let Harout know, let Harout know…"

"Swallow it," Harout shouted as he ran up to him, "Swallow it… so you don't suffocate, so you're not afraid of blood the next time… Swallow it!"

Harout lined up the boys at the edge of the valley and began whipping them with the horsehair rope. Rope? It was more than a rope—hissing as it came down and sliced through the air, ripping the young men's skin as it struck them, their veins exploding and the warm blood splattering on all sides. The boys moaned and writhed, but they held fast. They did not point fingers at each other. The villagers that had gathered watched but did not dare make a sound. Mekhak, whose son was at the front of the line, would groan and swear with each blow that landed on his child, "How dare you? Hurt my son, will you? Do you think he has no one to protect him?" As soon as Harout would turn around and look at the crowd of people, that shameless Mekhak would smile, "Do it, give them a good whipping so that they know not to make a mistake like that again." Harout would then turn back to the group of young boys and Mekhak would start all over again, "How dare you…" emboldened by the heavens.

He was taking little Harout home, with his ripped and bloodied shirt stuck to his back, while thinking about the first time he went to the outside world with Perch, when he had tugged at the arm of a waitress at a tavern in Erivan. "Take the boy and open his eyes," and he shoved Harout towards her. His eyes were not as closed, in all honesty, as Perch had assumed, and when he returned from the trip he could barely keep from telling his friends, "We've been hiding in Lipo's potato garden all this time, waiting for him to go to sleep so we could take turns with his wife. The city has sluts whose asses you can pinch even in daylight, imagine that!" Not to mention the fact that Lipo's eight children had tugged at his wife's nipples that they'd grown weak and blue, and she smelled more like a mother now than anything else. But the woman at the tavern… That's what a bitch should be like—young, pretty, with perky pink nipples, her skin smelling of perfumed oil…

As Little Harout walked ahead of him, Harout blamed himself. It was his fault. When he slaughtered an animal, gathered his harvest, returned from the outside world, collected dried twigs—he would always make a bundle and give it to little Harout to carry.

"Go give this to Nakhshun. The poor thing has no husband to care for her, and she's raising fatherless children."

"The whole village is full of women who have no husbands, she's raising two fatherless children, some of the others are raising twelve. Why is *she* the poor thing?" Little Harout would complain at the weight of the load.

"She's loyal, she deserves it."

"Why? Is Paytzar a slut? Is Maro a slut?"

"They're loyal to the joy they've experienced in the past. This one has not lived her life. It is very different to remain loyal to one's misfortune, it is a heroism of sorts."

"Huh," Little Harout would huff once he was out of earshot, "I know the kind of heroism you have in mind…"

Little Harout walked ahead of him, his head hanging low, wiping his nose with his arm from time to time to check whether the bleeding had stopped. Harout clapped the back of his neck affectionately.

"You little pup. Your whole height from head to toe isn't much, but you're already in trouble because of your pecker? If this is what you're like at fifteen, what are we going to do with you when you turn twenty?"

Harout would now sit on the wooden stairs every evening, stretching the long horsehairs as he weaved them and held them up in the air demonstratively with pride. But the horsehair rope did not seem to have much of an effect on the boys that were going through puberty in the village.

Sato would gather her eggs and arrange them in a basket, storing them in the cold and dark cellar. Whenever she saw Harout, she would try to rush him, "Hurry up, you have to go to the outside world… it's a shame if all these eggs spoil."

"Oh, Sato, Sato… your death is going to be a tough one!"

"Come on, brother. That is out of our hands—for now, God sees it fit for me to remain here."

"Ah," Harout would say, "If not for God, who would we blame for our sins?"

On that day, the mothers that had sons in the village lamented as they washed their children's bloodied shirts, poured the water into the river and curled up in terror at the burden of their thoughts. What if their son ended up being the culprit? They would have to take that slut in, for the child's sake.

Although it took Nakhshun a while to start accepting eggs as payment for her sheets, mostly so that she could pay Sato back, her daughters had been open to this currency from the very beginning for the services they provided at night, and eggs had turned into a standard of measure for the villagers.

"What a night it was, what a night…"

"Really? I mean, three eggs as usual, right?"

Or

"I bought a donkey—it cost me a thousand eggs!"

"Wow, a thousand eggs… Almost three hundred nights' worth… now *that's* expensive." But after that fight and the beating that Harout had doled out, people took it more seriously.

The women gathered in the morning and went to Varso's house, the emotions boiling in their hearts…

Even the clouds had not shouted that way when they ripped the sky apart… Their skirts were full of stones and they heaved those stones all over Varso's house. They broke her windows, smashed her wooden door and broke it off its hinges. Varso escaped from the house, the son of the king in her arms, and she hid in the *tonir*.

"Come out here, you heartless woman," the women screamed hysterically, "We know how our children slip away from their chores and their homes, they come to Varso's to listen to her stories…" But in reality, the son of the king had not been aware of the situation with Anahit, or the child in her belly. But before they had realized any of this, it had been too late. No matter whether the son of the king drowned in a marsh or was swallowed by a monster, the situation could not be undone. For seven days and seven nights, the son of the king and his horse sat, hungry and thirsty, in the darkness, on the warm ashes of the *tonir*, until Harout was able to take control of the women and send them home. On the seventh day, Varso came out of the *tonir*, her feet dusty, her eyes lost.

"Everyone," she said guiltily, "The son of the king has defeated forty monsters, and must defeat forty more. He was busy killing monsters, how was he to know what's been going on here?"

Poor Varso! She tried to do so much—she sent the son of the king from one world to the other, made him pass through the eye of a needle, gave him a heart forged with the scream of an angel—but nothing helped.

Nobody ever found out who had been the first, but… the fact was that one of the twins was pregnant. The women grabbed Sato by the throat. "Sato," they said, "You owe us a woolen shawl. You took that green shawl way back then but did not do the job. Now you have to pay us back somehow—save our boys from becoming the fathers of bastards and the husbands of whores. We can't take this humiliation any longer!"

Sato called the girl and said, "You're bringing a child without a father. What's the point? You don't have a father either—are you happy? At least you had Harout to support you… who's going to have this child's back? None of those whelps that resisted Harout's blows without confessing will take care of you or your child." She persuaded the girl and removed the bastard from her belly. But the girl did not feel well after that. Whether Sato had used falcon's claws, duck feet or whatever to scrape the womb, she had not disinfected her tools properly. She had either dipped them in vodka for too short a time, or she had ended up drinking the vodka herself. Who knew how Sato did things? Anyway, Harout wrapped the bleeding and unconscious Anahit in a carpet at night and put her on the back of his horse, then rode away.

"This late at night?" Sisak had held out a hand and pulled on the horse's rein, trying to push aside the steam breathing horse's face in an attempt to stop Harout from leaving. "There are all kinds of wolves and beasts in the mountains and valleys, they'll eat you up! She's going to die either way, and also…" he muttered to himself, "She's just a whore, isn't she?"

"Don't worry yourself. I've never been eaten by a wild animal and never will be," Harout had reassured him sullenly as he carried the carpet at night and took the girl to the outside world to save her. He had taken her wrapped in that carpet, and he brought her back the same way. They had told him it was too late.

"Too late? Don't let that bother you," the women had tried to reassure Harout, "Born that way, she was fated to die a death like this. The road that brings you must the one that you take back."

"They are so pretty…" Sato said, distancing herself from the blame, "Who would have let them stay pure?" And she barked at the young men, "Shame

[81]

on you… Damn you all… You're the victims of your own things." The villagers felt sorry for Nakhshun. "How could such girls come from a mother like her?"

"Nakhshun is the one to blame, of course," Onés tried to put together the cause and effect, "One shouldn't live such a chaste life, how can one be so pure? So God had to balance things out." And he started again. "Do you know whose granddaughters they are? Do you know what kind of a man Nakhshun's father was? He would give the poor forty sheep to eat every day. Do you know what kind of a man her betrothed was? He would teach forty children a day how to read. Do you know who her brother was? Her mother was a saint, a saint! And her, too! And what a great *knjru* she makes," Onés kept going, "You've never tasted *knjru* like that before."

And the people who heard him would imagine that it was a dish made of butterfly meat or snake milk. It did not matter at all.

"What happened to her father's gold? What happened to her betrothed's brains? Is any of that blood flowing in her? Is this the heir of someone who had money and brains?" the speaker of these words would point at Astghik, whose appearance would immediately make the boys brighten up and surround her, talking to her happily. The girl would talk to one of them with her eyes, another with her mouth, the movements of her hands would be directed at a third, the position of her back would communicate with a fourth… She would soak up their attention.

"They're young… that's what young people are like…"

But Onés got what he wanted in the end. He brought the village together for their first taste of *knjru* and the awe he knew it would cause. If only the villagers had known that Onés had never eaten any *knjru* in his life, nor had he even seen what it looked like. But he had heard about it throughout his journey here. The direction in which they had set out had not been the right one; there was only one lord when it came to life in these parts—the wind. It would swallow the sun and fall from the sky, blowing through the mountaintops and blow flakes from the ripped belly that would peel down at night and crunch under one's feet in the morning. The ground would take its time to become warm in the spring and the plants would grow slowly. In the summer, they would have already been boiled in the sun, in the autumn, they would be broken by the wind, and the early snow would upset them by pressing them against the soil. And they had to sustain themselves throughout their journey by eating the lichens growing on rocks. There would sometimes be worms or bugs on that moss and it would crunch beneath their teeth, and they would take pleasure in sucking up the juices as they chewed, but the bitterness of the lichens dulled it all—the flavor of the insects, as well as their desire to eat. Whenever one of them would heave from the strong bitterness of the moss, Nakhshun's father would always say, "If only we had some of that *knjru* you used to make, my child..." He had said this so often that Onés had virtually convinced himself—he *had* eaten that *knjru* before. In any case, by the time they had reached the village, they had gone through the same pain, and they were now a family.

Nakhshun rubbed the pot with sand and ash, then washed it under some pouring water. She placed it on the fire and filled it with oil. The oil crackled and droplets bounced here and there, blackening the spots where they landed. Nakhshun sprinkled some white flour into it, it baked and seared, reddened and sweated into the oil. Then she washed an egg and cracked it, beat it, whitened it, fluffed it and poured it into the flour. The egg hissed and swelled up immediately, startled by the heat. Nakhshun turned it over this way and that, reddening both sides, then placed it on the table.

"Enjoy..."

They ate it.

"It's like a regular omelet," they said, "Except it's with flour."

"But none of you make this here," Onés countered, "It's unique. It's milder, it doesn't cause a stomachache."

"Well," they said, "We put better ingredients into it. We make it with honey. But whether you use flour, honey or dog shit—isn't it an omelet in the end anyway? It's nothing original."

"Nothing in the world is original... We decide what's original, or we simply call something original. The way we look at something, *that* can be original."

"Oh, Onés, Onés... The crows would've plucked out your eyes a long time ago if not for that silver tongue of yours... If you can pretend that Nakhshun's children are Armenians, then it's even easier to make believe that an omelet is a *knjru*. What can we say to that?"

The shiny, green lizard would not have revealed itself if it had not slid down the back of the hardened red sorrel, spilling its dried seeds. But it had already made the mistake—it had slipped down to a rock and, sensing the bony large palm of the German approaching fast, its fluttering and flexible body was quickly absorbed by a crack in the stone, leaving the German with only the pain in his palm from slapping the hard surface. At first, he smiled with joy, peeking through the space between his fingers without lifting his hand from the rock. Seeing that his fingers and the stone had connected with no lizard in between, he began to wave his hand in the air, as if trying to shake off the pain and swelling. "It's all right," he consoled himself, "It was a small thing, barely a mouthful..." and he rushed to the lake to cool off his burning soles. "Oh, sun, you're still burning brightly. Eternity has not tired you, eclipses have not damaged you, you still shine bright. Go to sleep for a couple of minutes, the deserts want to live too. Their scorched sand is burning, and I'm walking all over it..." the German hopped forward as he burned his feet in the sun and directed this plea towards the sun. He would take a few steps, then run back to the lake and drench his feet, a blissful expression on his face, before starting to walk along the shore once again... The white-hot sand and pebbles beneath his feet would once again prove too much, and he would rush back to the lake... There were days when he was luckier—he would sometimes find a sandy piece of fish on the shore, ripped apart by the beaks of ravens, and he would wave it in the air and emit shouts of joy, showing it to his friends. But the ravens must have been hungry when they had come today—they had consumed the fish completely, or the waves had been weak and unable to overturn the bottom of the lake onto the shore. It was yellow everywhere and sunny, even where the sky was supposed to be blue and the soil black.

Policeman Vardanyan, his assistant Poghos, and Sergo the driver were hidden in the truck, laughter hanging on their lips as they enjoyed the tribulations of their prisoner.

"Call him," the driver called out, "Call him over here before the frogs eat him."

Poghos bent two of his fingers into his palm and raised his forefinger and pinky to his mouth. He curled his tongue and the whistle rang out loudly in the air.

The German understood the meaning of the whistle correctly. He grabbed his reddened forehead in one hand and snatched the paper hat he had made off the camelthorn bush where it had settled after the wind had blown it off his head. He rushed up towards them. Stubbing his toe against a rock and causing it to bleed, he thought to himself that this country had been made a completely different way from the others—the bones had come first, then the rest… He could hear the call of groundwater as it flowed between the roots of the rocks and rubbed against them. Its cold sighing was enough to cool only the dry, white rocks. The German crawled on his hands and looked between the rocks, convinced that at any moment he would be able to find the water scratching against the rocks or come across another lizard—maybe even a snake, if he was lucky.

As he walked and boiled under the sun, Hans stretched his hand to his breast pocket and felt around there, sensing the roughness of the paper, and he continued to fight the sun with a happy smile. There would be moments—these happened mostly at night—when he would take out the photograph he had in that pocket, the one with the two children and the woman with the tired eyes, and lift it up to his lips with a joyful smile, with no consideration for who ended up receiving his kiss in the darkness of the night. It was a photo of his family, one he had managed to rescue from several interrogations, beatings and deprivations, one that had been with him throughout the war, it had been taken prisoner with him and stubbornly battled the Caucasus sun and the Armenian rocks.

When he felt the cold, the soft touch on his leg which was burning on a rock, he looked down and saw a frog on his foot and his heart exploded with joy. That frog was as much a consolation to him at that moment as a prayer in a predicament without escape. Crouching carefully, he brought his palm closer. Then he stood up triumphantly, holding on to the frog by the leg and showing his prey off to his friends. The prisoners of war standing at the foot of the mountain had probably not even had a good look at what he was holding, but they realized that it was food and they responded with much shouting. One of them even began to pluck dry twigs and break them for the fire that was to be started.

"Fritz… Fritz…" Sergo called out and gestured him over with a finger. The prisoner changed direction and came closer. The driver snapped off the paper hat from his head, took it apart and smoothed the paper, then held out another newspaper, *Pravda*, to the German and said mockingly, "Here, make a Russian hat for yourself," as he shook the other paper, in Armenian, and held it before his eyes.

"Let's do something to pass the time," he justified his actions before the policeman that was looking at him in surprise, "At least look at some of these pictures."

The prisoner stood there for a moment, pointing a finger into his open mouth and then rubbing his hand on his chest.

"What's he saying? Is he hungry?"

"No," Poghos seemed to have guessed it, "He must be thirsty."

"Come on, man," policeman Vardanyan said, looking at the man in surprise, "Look out there—a whole sea of water to drink!"

The prisoner looked in amazement at the lake, and then the hand that was pointing to it.

"The ones they have back home are saltwater," the policeman explained, glancing at his comrades, and he cupped his hands like a ladle and first held them out in the direction of the lake, then lifted them into the air and to his mouth, explaining to the prisoner that he could drink that water.

Did the prisoner understand that the lake held fresh water, or did he think they were mocking him? In any case, he looked in terror at the rocks all around him and imagined that he would have to walk over them once again to get to the lake, after which he seemed to get over his thirst quickly. The policeman picked up a cup from the car and walked to the lake as he intimidated the stones on the shore beneath the soles of his new boots. He walked into the lake up the point where his boots allowed, lowered the metallic cup into the water and demonstratively drank from it. Then he filled it again and brought it over for the prisoner. As the surprised prisoner drank the water, the policeman happily stamped his feet on the ground in order to free himself of a piece of moss.

"Get back to work now," he said to the prisoner, picking up the cup that he held out and looking sadly at the frog still hanging by its leg from the man's hand.

The Germans could not believe what they saw around themselves. The bony waves, white like an old scar, would crash against each other as they rolled out into the visible eternity. The rocks were immortal and unbearable, driven deep into the heart of the soil like an insult, dense, unable to be swallowed... Innumerable stones, with thorns sticking out in parts from their cracked lips, lizards slipping in and out of them, creating the illusion that the rocks were sticking out their tongues. The red seeds of the dried sorrels had stuck to the surfaces of the slabs. "*Schnell, schnell,*" the policeman called out from below, and the prisoners of war did not dare to sit down, take a break, or catch their breaths.

"Why are we in this desert, anyway?" Poghos was upset. "Wasn't there any other land that needed clearing?"

"The orders say to clear out this land."

"Don't the orders say we have to uproot that mountain?" the driver mumbled.

"We'll do that too if we have to," the policeman snapped.

The sun pierced them with such hostility that they forgot all the good things it had done to them so far. The driver put his large palms on his head in order to protect it and ran to the car. The policemen did not last long either, they sought protection in the shade of the car and only stepped outside once in a while, glancing over at the prisoners and shouting the only word they knew in a menacing tone—*schnell.* The sun had become unbearable and even a love for one's homeland no longer helped one swallow the baked air.

"If you were to ask me," the driver Sergo proposed, tying the corners of his wet handkerchief and pulling it across the top of his head like a diadem, "We should help them, finish up quickly, and go."

"Help them? This isn't a one-hour job, or even a one-day job... We're not going to relieve them of the fact that they're prisoners, are we?" Poghos took out a map from his pocket, spread it out on the ground and began to examine it with suspicion. "Could we perhaps have misunderstood the instructions?"

The driver stretched his neck towards the map.

"Put that away," Vardanyan said with disdain, "We've all grown up in these parts. Do you think we need maps to know where we've been assigned our task?"

The screaming of the prisoners became blended with the sound of rolling rocks. The three of them leaped out of the shadows to see what had happened. Just then, one of the prisoners came down with a rolling boulder and slammed into the wheels of the truck.

"Is he dead?" the driver asked fearfully.

"I don't know... I guess so..." the policeman mumbled. He looked at the prisoners that stood petrified among the white rocks on the hillside.

"Come down from there," he gestured with his hand, "That's enough for today…"

The driver walked up to the car.

"I'll move the car a bit…"

"We should bury this one, I guess," Vardanyan proposed, indicating the corpse with his head.

"How?" Poghos looked at the rocks all around them, "Do you even see a handful of soil?"

"We can cover him with stones."

"Tell them to do it," Vardanyan indicated to the prisoners with his head.

The driver gestured with arms and legs, explaining to the prisoners that they had to bury the corpse under a pile of stones. Unsure of whether they had understood him, he began to pick up some rocks from the ground.

"Otherwise, the wolves are going to have a feast tonight," he threatened in Armenian, shocked by what had happened.

The prisoners walked up timidly, one of them felt for a pulse on their fallen friend and shook his head, a painful expression on his face. They found a pit of sorts not too far away and they dragged him over there, rolled him in and, shuddering, begin to pick up small stones from the ground and pour them on him.

"*Schnell*," the policeman pointed at the back of the truck, and the prisoners dragged themselves over, grabbing the railing to pull themselves on board.

The following day, when the prisoners came to continue their work, the wind had joined the sun and it was impossible to breathe the sticky air, because the wind seemed to snatch it from one's mouth.

The prisoners were agitated, whispering something to themselves, and the wind tore their words—already incomprehensible in their foreign language—to unfathomable bits. One cannot understand anything when there is wind because, besides dissipating all words here and there, it also adds its own noise to all the sounds. No matter how hard the policeman strained his ears, he could not hear anything from the shreds of half-drowned conversation that reached him.

"What's wrong with them? You haven't given them any vodka, have you?" he was upset and stuck his mouth to his assistant's ear as he spoke, in order to make sure that the wind would not carry his words away.

"Where would I get vodka from?" his assistant shouted back into his ear, "We would be drinking it now, if I had any vodka."

"So why are they so agitated?" Vardanyan said, the palms of his hands trying to protect his words this time.

"The corpse we buried yesterday is gone. It's disappeared... that must be why."

"What do you mean, disappeared?" Vardanyan shouted right into the wind and rushed over to check.

"Well, what did you expect?" the driver Sergo shook his head sadly, "When the wolves find something to eat, they're going to drag it away, aren't they?"

The prisoners worked for more than a month to clear the place of rocks and expose the soil underneath. But the wind would bring back stones overnight to the areas they had cleared during the day, or the rocks would roll themselves into place and conquer new territory, exposing the roots of the moss covering them and the nests of insects for the sun to burn the following day. When the prisoners would arrive, they would tense with anger upon seeing a whole pyramid of new rocks where only one had stood the previous day... And everything would start once again—endlessly and without a break, like the pointless and incessant running of a hamster in a wheel.

"Listen," Poghos whispered into the driver's ear one day, "Have you noticed any changes in these prisoners?"

"No. What do you mean?"

"I think that one's a little fatter now."

"Oh, come on..." Sergo guffawed, "With the food you're giving him..."

"I swear... Look at this young one. His fingers seem thicker, and so does his neck. Otherwise these ones would have fallen prey to the wolves on their very first day, like that other one did."

Vardanyan got out of the car.

"Where do you get the energy to talk so much in this heat?" he said, walking up to them.

"If only you'd heard what your friend hear is saying," the driver mocked.

"What's he saying?"

"He says we've given these prisoners so much *khash* and barbecue that they've put on weight."

"Of course they've put on weight," Vardanyan joined in on the fun, "They'll all have beer bellies soon."

He walked ahead and, without turning around, called back to his comrades.

"The beach is sandier on the other side. You watch over them, I'm going for a swim since the wind has died down a bit." And he left, undoing the buttons of his shirt as he walked.

"What are we, your servants?" his assistant settled down into a space with sparse grass, in the shadow of the vehicle. "I'm going to take a nap. That kid of ours wasn't well last night, I didn't get any sleep."

Twenty minutes had barely gone by when Vardanyan ran back in panic.

"You'll never believe what I've found!"

"A crock of gold," the assistant, leaning on his elbows and still sleepy, was now mocking his boss.

"A grave!" Vardanyan announced with a scream.

"But why are you so scared? This is ancient land… you'll probably come across all kinds of graves and tombstones if you dig a little anywhere," Sergo the driver quipped.

"But this isn't an old one, see? It's a new grave, it's recent."

"How do you know?"

"I even know where the tombstone was made… it's the work of Hrach from Gavar. He's the only one who makes cross-stones in these parts."

"So now you're going to get Hrach in trouble? So many priests have been exiled… All that we have left are Hrach's cross-stones, and you're going to make sure we lose them too," the driver said with disdain.

"This isn't about Hrach," Vardanyan took offense at that, "That's not what I'm saying. If this is a new grave, then there are people living around here. If that's the case, why are we torturing ourselves in this sun and fiery heat?"

"No way…" the assistant now sat up in the grass, "Who could live in secret from the Soviet authorities? We were born and raised in these parts. Wouldn't we know? It might just be the grave of a suicide, or something…"

"Suicides' graves used to be separate from the others in the old days. They would even bury them face down…" Sergo the driver made the sign of the cross in his mind and thought "God forbid such things from happening…"

"Well that's what I'm saying. Someone must have brought them here and secretly buried them… so that the wolves could howl at their grave."

"But if the person had spat on the heavens by giving up the life that was given to him, would you sculpt a cross on their gravestone?" the thought of the secret grave made Vardanyan turn back and look in its general direction.

The grave that had been discovered turned into an obsession for Vardanyan. It followed him everywhere like his own shadow. It was even more than a shadow because shadows disappear when the sun sets, you get some freedom from them at night at the very least. But the grave pursued him day and night—it was with him, in his head. In all these rocks, why did that one stone bother him so much—because it had a particular shape and features? Did he not understand that time itself was misshapen, and what was shape itself—a border, a cage? These eternal rocks, the ossified time that the mountains represented—did they not deserve the same attention by mankind as this little stone that had been given a particular interpretation? He had no answer to this question and rushed to the gravestone that had grown like a spur in the side of the mountain. What was driving him to that grave? The charm of touching a special kind of solitude? Was it mere curiosity? Was it the charm of the cross-stone? Or was it a sense of professional concern at the thought that something had happened in the area without his supervision or knowledge?

"Nobody has lived in these parts for hundreds of years. When did you get here? When did you die?" he spoke to the cross-stone in his thoughts. He would bring the prisoners of war there and order them to clear the territory of rocks. He would shout "*Schnell*," loudly a couple of times and then go over to examine the gravestone. "Who are you, my good fellow?" he would say, walking around the stone. "When did you live? When did you die? Are you a woman, or a man? Old, or a child? No years, no images... What am I supposed to do with you?" He would examine the cross-stone from various angles, "Whose bones are growing whiter under your weight, o blessed stone?"

His comrades made fun of him. As soon as he turned to head to the stone, his assistant would poke Sergo in the ribs.

"He's off to see his mistress," and he would laugh silently.

"Vardanyan," Sergo would call after him, smiling, "When are the two of you going to get married so that we can be done with this?"

But Vardanyan had no appetite for that kind of humor and he paid them no heed. His curiosity was killing him. He even went all the way to Bayazet and found Hrach's house, but the sculptor had neatly arranged all his tools beneath a wall and died a month earlier. He returned, unsatisfied. "Who are you, o emptiness of mine, how can you exist without me?" and he would kneel next to the cross-stone and helplessly put his palm on the slab. He had even come here several times in the dark—in secret from everyone else and ignoring the roaming jackals—because he had been afraid that spending too much time here during the day could mean that witnesses, or even his comrades, would deliver this news to the relevant instances, and he would be accused of respecting the cross, a religious symbol. He examined the shadow cast by the stone at different times of the day, the cracks on the slab, the moss covering parts of it—none of it made sense to him. Nothing eased his suffering. The only thing that suggested a human connection to it was the clay incense pot turned upside down in its right corner. But what could the fire-blackened clay tell him?

On all of the following days without exception, Vardanyan put the prisoners of war to work as soon as they arrived by shouting "*Schnell!*" and, as soon as he noticed his comrades dozing off from the heat in the shadow of the vehicle, he would secretly run to take a look at the gravestone. This was a source of amusement for the driver Sergo but an issue of concern for Poghos—"Has he lost his mind?"

On that particular day, Vardanyan ran back to his comrades and sat down next to them, staring in fear.

"I swear," the driver laughed, "It's no fun job being a policeman—one of you guys sees a gravestone, the other imagines that the prisoners are putting on weight."

Sergo, lazy from the heat, got up, brought back a package from the car and opened it.

"I'm having lunch," he declared with a shout. He laid a newspaper on the ground and arranged his food on it.

"I believe that now," Vardanyan suddenly exclaimed, "I believe that they've put on weight. Someone is secretly feeding them. There are people living in these parts, there are people…"

"Well, you should check up on that," Sergo yawned mockingly, "Especially since you're the one with the gun."

"Poghos has a gun too… right, Poghos?" Vardanyan poked his dozing assistant, "I'll give mine too. You'll have two pistols. You'll stay here and check things out."

"Hey! I told you—my child is ill and didn't let me sleep a wink at night…"

"Don't worry. I'll go to your house to check on your family. I'll arrange for a doctor and some candy for your kid. I'll tell them not to expect you tonight. We'll be back with the rest of the guys in the morning."

"Yeah? Well, I'm in no mood for jokes like this… Let me take a nap. I got to sleep at four in the morning and had to be up at six."

"I'm not joking. The Party needs this."

"If the Party needs it, you can stay and do it."

"What? I'll report to our superiors. I'll let everyone know that you did not carry out the Party's orders."

The assistant shot up from where he was laying and sat upright.

"Vardanyan *jan*," he said, frightened, "You seem to have forgotten that there were wolves in these part that dragged away that dead body. Who cares about the prisoner? He was one of Hitler's men. But I am a father of three!"

"The Fatherland demands an explanation… You have to stay here and find out how the prisoners are putting on weight."

The driver felt sorry for Poghos.

"Well, we can leave the prisoners too… I mean, why should we have to drive them back and forth every day? That'll save us some trouble and it means that Poghos won't be all alone out here."

"I can't allow that," Vardanyan disagreed, "I have to sign documents to take them out and them sign others to let them back in."

"Don't be scared," Sergo turned to Poghos and encouraged him, "There are no large animals in these parts. Just bears and wolves… Oh, and one piece of advice. Don't wait for the wolves to eat you—you eat them first…"

As he said the word "eat", Sergo finished wrapping his *lavash* tightly to make sure that nothing fell out of the sandwich, and he bit in with great appetite, pretending to be a hungry wolf.

The policemen joined him, making sandwiches of pickles and boiled potatoes.

"Shouldn't we give them any sandwiches?" Sergo proposed, indicating to the prisoners, "We can't finish all this, nor can we take it back with us. If we don't finish the eggs, they'll go bad."

"No sandwiches… Let them work and make up for Hitler's sins," Vardanyan said angrily, pulling the pickles and boiled eggs in his direction. "I like this food, I'll finish it."

"Oh, Vardanyan, Vardanyan," the driver got to his feet, looked with compassion at the prisoners and appeared dumbstruck. He sat down again suddenly. Then he got to his feet once more. He looked out again.

"Someone was waving from the cave!"

"Really?" Vardanyan put a hand on his weapon and immediately got to his feet. "*Schnell! Schnell!* Get down here!" he shouted. And he almost fainted. The prisoners were gone, they had disappeared.

They were forced to bring out the hunting dogs.

The hunchbacked tinsmith stood in front of Sato's door at noon sharp, when the rays of the sun had extended deep to examine the heart of the wet moss to the bottom of the valley. Sato had so many plates with holes that needed tinning over, that the thought did not even cross her mind—"So far, not a single snake has crawled nor has a chicken flown over the border of this village—how did this stranger get here?" As the hunchback laid out his instruments on the rocks warmed by the sun, Sato stood at the top of the Spring and, arms akimbo, shouted to the women of the village to bring their plates with holes. When several women had already gathered, they realized that the stranger spoke a language that was neither Turkish, nor Arabic, nor Farsi. And that was when the women grew afraid, because they had no idea why he had appeared there. The news got to Harout.

"He must be Russian," Sato concluded, calmed by Harout's arrival.

"*Rus, Rus…*" the tinsmith was excited.

Harout called out to Vazgen.

"You'd met a Russian general on your journey here, and you'd said you know how to laugh in Russian. Can you speak the language?"

"Of course I do!"

"Well then, come and ask this man how much he will take to cover the holes of our plates with tin."

"I can't," Vazgen shouted back from the depths of his garden, "I only know a couple of words, and I'm saving those for our own plates."

The women went back and forth with their plates, laughing, joking and poking each other with each joke, as they piled up the items next to the tinsmith. The Russian was working hard and Sato thought that it would be good to serve him a meal. "I have what matters most—vodka!" She thought first about making him an omelet, but then changed her mind.

This man was a guest from another country—she would slaughter one of her poultry.

Her noisy rooster made for a delicious dish with rice. Sato sat down to eat with Harout and the tinsmith. There were no toasts. Sato placed some of the rice, still crackling in the oil, in front of the guest. Harout kept pouring shot after shot of vodka. But both of them felt a kind of fear inside—who was this tinsmith? After the meal, the tinsmith took a nap while Harout finished some chores and prepared to take him to the outside world—"It must be tough for you to carry those instruments on your hunched back. I'll take you in my cart," he had said, partly using words, partly through active gestures with his hands and feet. Sato gave a look confirming Harout's words and went about her own tasks till the cart came.

At sunset, the cart stood near Sato's door. He waited till the tinsmith meticulously arranged his instruments and then took the man out of the village. He did not kill him. He simply tied up his hands and legs and threw him in the well of the potato field.

Harout kept delaying his next trip to the outside world. Sato had gathered her eggs and did not know what to do. She had caught some hens and was plucking the feathers on their bellies so that part of their bodies would cool and they would feel the warmth of the eggs they laid, setting off a maternal instinct in them that would lead them to brood. Just then, the children stormed into her house, panting.

"Sato... Sato, come quickly, Varso is delirious, she might be dying!"

Sato did not immediately stop what she was doing because she had just seen Varso leaning on a stone wall, her thick feet set apart as she puffed on her pipe. Sato simply turned her head towards the children and saw how a rooster in the middle of the yard had climbed on top of a hen and had pressed its head to the ground, pecking it. She watched them until the rooster spread its wings and beat the air with its feathers, then got off the other bird. Then she calmly looked at the impatient children, released the hen that had been clucking in her arms, its breast already mercilessly exposed like a mountain peak after the summer thaw, and she waved her hands to free them of the attached feathers. In the end, she rubbed her hands—wiser because of all the wrinkles on them, as opposed to her pocked face—on her belly.

"It's all right, children," she said, groaning as she moved her old knees, "Varso is past ninety years old and is within touching distance of a hundred. Dying is a better option for her now."

"But the story—it's not finished yet! The son of the king is facing a tall mountain. There's a mirror in his breast pocket that will turn into a huge lake when he throws it. He has a comb that will turn into a dense forest when he throws it. He has a sword too—a magic one that he can use to slice the mountain in two. But he's waiting for his horse to come so that they can discuss it together... Varso can't die now!"

"Yeah? But where's the horse?"

"It went to get a drink of water but got lost in a thorny bush. Varso has to rescue it!"

"I pity the horse that has to rely on Varso to get it out of a thorny bush!"

With her simple and prolonged story, Varso had kept the imagination of the village for so many years—almost a lifetime!

"I wonder what's going to happen in the end," the people said to each other.

"What do you think is going to happen? The boy is going to behead the monster."

"But so many stories end that way. There's nothing new there."

"So why can't the same thing happen in this story? Aren't all stories the same?"

"If this were like other stories it would have ended by now. This one is different."

When the children or someone else in the house was late in returning from an errand, the mothers would be worried, "I wonder what happened to him? It's like the horse in Varso's story," they would say. When they saw Varso in the village, everyone would joke,

"Varso, what happened to the son of the king? Is he still traveling?"

"Yes, he is," she would confirm, blowing smoke from her pipe into the air and then closely examining the cloud she had created.

"Come on... He could have used all this time to conquer one kingdom, establish another, get married, have ten children, and behead the dragon..."

"But why should he do everything *your* way?" Varso would joke, "Why should he do what you want? You can do all that yourself, if that is what you desire. He's a free man. He can go where he likes and do what he wants."

"Yes, sister, but the roads in this story have stretched out so much... can a story last this long? When is it going to end?"

"Ah," Varso would wave her hand contemptuously, "Go about your work... The end will come even if we're no longer around to see it."

"Oh, Varso, Varso... making up all kinds of lies."

"And why not? Why can't I mix in my own portion of lies to this deceitful life? What would that change?"

Before she had even walked in, Sato picked up the smell of death in the doorway and, wrinkling her nose at the bitterness that had stuck to her palate, she coughed. She blinked her eyes so that they would get used to the darkness indoors after the bright sunlight outside, and then she whispered, "Run and call Harout."

Harout took out a pomegranate from a box on the tuffet—he had given one of these to Nakhshun as a gift the last time he had come from the outside world—and he put it into his inner pocket before leaving. The children had surrounded the wooden tuffet and were begging her, "Varso *jan*, we've waited so long, please don't die without telling us how it ends, please tell us how it ends before you..."

"Oof," Varso groaned, exhausted by the weight of her own soul.

Seeing Harout, her neighbor walked up.

"We brought her back," she whispered into his ear.

"Why?" Harout imagined for a moment all the screaming and shouting, the crying and lamentation that was coming from Varso's tormented soul, stuck in thorny bushes, "The Turks ruined this poor woman's life, and you ruined her death. Couldn't you have let her live out that last moment in peace?"

"I don't know," the woman hung her shoulders, embarrassed at the mistake she had made, "The children wanted to know the end of the story, and she was leaving without telling them."

The villagers, her neighbors, all lined up around Varso and were mourning the old woman that was still alive. After all, what would be the point of doing it later? Varso had to see how much she was worth while she was still there.

"Varso *jan*, isn't there anything you would like to say to us?" Vaghinak the shepherd silenced the sobbing women with a stern look.

"What would I say?"

"Varso *jan*, just in case—God forbid—something were to happen to you... allow me to inherit the story from you. Give me the right to tell everyone how it ends."

"Brother, you have your shepherd's staff, your sheep... are you the best person to tell this story?'

"Well, if you want to know the truth, Varso *jan*, you're really putting the king's middle son through a lot," Vaghinak grew angry, "Why should he become a prisoner of the monster, slice the mountain into two, defeat this one or that one? He needs to enjoy life! Let me inherit the story, I'll make it much richer. I'll give that kid wings—and his horse, too! Let them both soar up into the sky."

"I can't," Varso suddenly rejected him, wiping the cold sweat of death off her forehead, "We need that boy to be on land."

"Think about it, Varso *jan*," the neighbor would not give up, "I'll give our boy divine powers. He can stay on land if he wants to, or fly into the air when he wishes."

"What a brain you have," Varso praised him in a wheezy voice between moans, "Go and make up any another story that comes to your mind."

"But it is such a shame to lose this one. We've heard it all these years, we've grown and the story had grown with us... Varso *jan*, listen to me, this is already out there, why should anyone start a new one?"

"If you're just a listener and your heart aches because you can't bear the thought of parting with the story, think about me—I'm the one who made it up. I've been telling this story all these years and I've brought it up to this point. Now you want me to give it to you and ruin it?"

"That won't do, Varso *jan*... This story is as much ours as it is yours. If you're not going to pass it on to anyone, tell us how it ends."

"I will... what's the hurry?"

"But when?"

Harout walked up and looked at the old woman's bed. He recognized the sheet as being Nakhshun's work. He took the pomegranate and carefully rolled it to Varso's weak hands, and he said with a sigh,

"Varso *jan*..."

"Varsenik..." for the first time since she had come to the village, she asked them to use her full name. "From now on, call me Varsenik," she ordered Harout as he stood by her bed.

"Varsenik," Harout repeated, the unfamiliar word causing a strange taste in his mouth, "Varsenik *jan*, think of these poor children. They are hanging their heads and waiting for you. Tell them how it ends and let them go... Or let each of them imagine an ending for themselves. Think of the poor kids!"

"No," Varso said, "The son of the king suffered a lot... Even if he never complained, the poor thing, he's only human... Those rocky paths wore him down. I'll take him with me, he can finally get some rest."

"Varsenik... you are not a child, nor am I. If you don't want everyone to know, reveal it only to me. The story has been with us all this time, shouldn't we get to know how it ends? Look at these children. Look at how they have hung their heads as they stare at your mouth. Tell us what happens."

"I will," Varso said confidently, "But put me in your cart and take me to the lake just once."

Harout, surprised, looked hesitantly around him.

"Varsenik," he laughed, "If not for these loudmouthed women, you'd already be at God's feet now. You're on the verge of dying, why do you want me to take you anywhere?"

"As you wish," Varso barely managed to say, but said confidently.

"Brother Harout," the children turned to him, "If it makes no difference to her isn't it all the same to you? At least that way we'll know how the story ends."

"It's the last wish of the dying," the women insisted.

Harout looked at Varso and said, "Fine." He picked her up, mattress and all, and placed her in the cart, which he then turned towards the lake. For a moment, when the cart's wheels crunched over some rocks, Varso stuck her head up and looked proudly at everyone, satisfied that she had earned the right to leave the village, and then her head crashed back on to her pillow.

"Damn that Varso," the shepherd sighed as they left, "She's going to tell Harout the ending. Who are we for her to trust us with such power?"

Slimy moss, lake pebbles covered with holes and lime... small waves ripped by the wind tried stubbornly to slap against the slabs and pick off the lichens. In its depths, the cold and uneasy waters of the lake were fighting with the wind—the wind would drag a wave up and bite into the water like a witch that would chew on lead. The cliff on the shore had turned into a mass of shards that would later madly roll down to the lake, digging into its bottom, but stood for the moment bare and smooth, slapped about by the waves, the gulls gathered between the shards...

"Look up the sky—there's so much there... look down here—there's so much there..." Varso had first lifted an arm towards the sky and then hung it towards the lake. "But all that we inherited from God's possessions is solitude." Varso had forgotten that she was with Harout. She kept staring at Lake Sevan and talking to herself.

"Varsenik, are you a pagan?" Harout was surprised, "Are you praying to the lake?"

"This isn't a lake, Harout *jan*. This is what is left of Noah's flood. This is the last sip of God's wrath... Do you know why? Because there are still sins on the earth that need to be washed away. There are still things that need to be drowned... That bloody sin of ours that must be washed away..."

"Oh, poor, naïve Varsenik... what can the lake do?"

"Blood can be washed in water," the old woman sighed, "Blood has always been washed in water."

"When a single person is naïve, Varsenik, that can come across as cute. But when a whole bunch people are that innocent then this is a significant disadvantage. And our mistake has been that we believe that blood is washed away, while in reality it is drunk by others," Harout said, "And so, Varsenik *jan*, it is time for the ending to your story—what happens to the son of the king?"

"I don't know, I swear, Harout *jan*..." Varso swore with a fist on her chest, "If I'd known all that, I wouldn't be Varsenik, I would be the Lord our God." Varso closed her eyes, and she was gone, her soul carrying all the suffering and torment that she had received in return for being a child of God.

Harout turned the cart around and walked to the village, a new duty on his shoulders now. "Damn you, Varso... what have you done? Could you have made things any more difficult for me?" Who knows whether Varso had done a good deed or a bad one by passing on the duty of the story to him? From the day Varso had arrived to this one, the son of the king was still twenty years old, just as he had been back then. Nobody thought of asking, "Varso, so many people were born and died over these years, why isn't the king's middle son growing any older?" So it was up to Harout to age the prince, "The villagers all think that Varso told me how the story ends... I need to come up with an ending, otherwise the poor things will be disappointed." If he failed, he would take the option that

Varso had chosen, "I will continue telling the story, making it longer and longer... pretending that this ending was not like the others, that it was more powerful and needed a lot more effort to get to, the prince had to keep going, the story needed more time."

Seated at the table for the memorial meal, when people were mourning and remembering Varso, telling stories of their memories of her and incidents related to her, while others would mourn with sighs or "Oh"-s , Yero suddenly slammed the cup of mourning down on the table after she had drunk from it and began to cry loudly. And the people understood—after all, who else but Yero had the most right to cry? She had so much for which to weep, let her cry it out.

"Yero *jan*," Bavakan felt sorry for her, seeing how the blood had flowed to her capillaries and suffocated the whites of her eyes, and tried to bring her attention back to the living, "How's your husband?"

"He's fine, I'm sure, why wouldn't he be? Living in the house his father made, eating the food that comes from his wife's work. All he's thought about his whole life is his pecker, why wouldn't he be fine?"

"Well, that's good, that's good... How are the two of you doing now? You seem to be doing well."

"Yes," Yero replied, her voice moist with tears, "As long as I'm the one bearing his burden, we're fine. He provides evidence of how much he loves me four or five times a day." She recalled her paternal uncle Vahan, who had had four boys. "May those Turks die; may they see no days of good fortune. They set the house on fire at night and barbecued a whole family that was smiling in their sleep." When that uncle was asked about his daughters-in-law, he would say about the eldest one, "Oh God forbid, I wouldn't wish such a daughter-in-law on the enemy. The middle one? There's nothing human about her. The third one? Not like the others, but still not quite right. The fourth one is a good woman; you can't say anything bad about her." Here, her uncle would sigh, "They're all gone..."

Yero stepped outside and looked for Harout among the people that had gathered. She saw him in the depths of the garden, talking to Sato. As she walked up to them, she heard, "I've gathered her clothes into a bundle. They're in your cart." Sato said, "When you go out into the world, put them down somewhere, or give them to someone, it'll be a good deed... someone else can wear them."

"Give me her worry beads," Harout said, "She was a good woman, I want to have a memento."

Sato took out the worry beads from her bosom. "It's amber," Sato said, holding the beads out to Harout, "She had brought it with her from that other life." Harout took it, rolled a few of the beads onto each other and then sighed, putting it into his pocket. Yero gestured to Harout and took him to a wall where two women were quickly collecting the dried buttermilk so that it would not gather dust from the feet of the people that were coming and going. She said,

"Harout *jan*, I've had my fill of crying. It's difficult, very difficult, to break free from the past. Then I told myself, 'Why are you crying? It's the one without a past that should be crying. Whether good or bad, I've lived my life, I've left something behind...' Don't you think I'm right?"

"You're right. Life always leaves you with something—wrinkles on those that were happy, but they run deeper on the other ones..."

"I don't have wrinkles," Yero ran a hand over her sunburnt face.

"You don't," Harout confirmed, "You're a pretty woman."

"So tell me, Harout. Should I have a child with you, or with Musayel's son?"

"The vodka has gone to her head," the woman collecting the dried buttermilk giggled to themselves although, on the other hand, one swig of the stuff would not have led to such thoughts. And so they slowed their work and listened in, although pretending they did not intend to do so.

"Musayel's the better choice," Harout pretended to joke and left, mingling with the men standing at the wall that were talking about the deceased and discussing aspects of her life that had not been considered earlier.

"She lived in our village for such a long time, but she never considered us family. She never made us a 'lady's navel' so that we could taste what it was like," Vasil complained, approaching Harout.

"Come on, man," Harout defended Varso, "Do you have to eat it to imagine what it's like?"

"I mean, with the stories she cooked up, I can only imagine how well she baked!" someone else confirmed.

"What stories? It was all about a single horse in the end, wasn't it? I mean, if you're making up a story, why not make it about ten horses? She had us all hanging on to find about that one young man and that single horse. Was that nice of her?" Vasil was unforgiving.

At that moment, Yero walked up to the men and cast an offended glance at Harout, then spat out, "You can keep Musayel… Why would I take on another old man, am I not suffering enough at the hands of the one I have? You tell me one thing—should I have a girl, or a boy?"

"A child is a child, it doesn't matter. What matters is that the child has good luck, a father and a mother."

"Fine. Whatever God gives me, then…" Yero agreed, "But Harout *jan*, it doesn't matter if you go up to the heavens and come down again, you're not going to be able to stop me. I'll take what I want."

"Get rid of that chip on your shoulder. I would not suggest going ahead with this."

"Who's asking you, anyway?" Yero clicked her tongue and said in a cranky voice before she moved away, leaving the men confused.

"What was that all about, Harout, has that woman gone crazy?" Sisak asked, laughing.

"Come on now…" Vazgen smiled forgivingly, "She's an old woman, she's had something to drink… We should allow her to let it all come out."

On the following day, the people were gathering to go to Varso's grave when Yero showed up again and stuck tightly to Harout.

"Harout… Harout, my brother Harout… I've done it." Her self-satisfied voice rang out so loudly that the people walking in front turned around and looked questioningly at Harout.

"Yeran," Harout whispered through gritted teeth, "You've suffered a lot. I want you to think hard about how you're behaving. Why are you talking so loudly?"

"I did it… last night…" she rolled her eyes contentedly and tried to whisper into Harout's ear, "I didn't sleep a wink all night, thinking—should I do it or shouldn't I? Should I do it, or shouldn't I? Then I said to myself, 'Yeran, you've had your share of breast milk in this life, you can go ahead and kill that man.' To be honest, I was a bit afraid of God, I was thinking…"

"But why kill him? If you were to forget about him, no longer think about him, wouldn't that be a sort of death for him too? Do people have to be separated by a layer of soil for one of them to be dead? How is forgetting about someone any different that covering them with soil? It is time, after all, that piles on to a person with each day, like a handful of soil…"

"I could no longer bear it, Harout *jan*, I reached for the knife…"

"What? Who've you killed?" the women walking in front could bear it no longer and turned around.

The shepherd's underage daughter, holding the incense and matches in her hand, opened her eyes wide —"Who've you killed?"

"Yeran, you've humiliated me," Harout whispered and stopped the procession to make an announcement, "We have to gather in the evening. We'll gather, there is something we need to discuss."

That night, Harout gathered the people in the village and said, "All this time, I've never asked you who you were, where you came from, what you want, who your God is, to whom do you pray… And I will not ask it now. But, at dawn, some people will show up with guns and other weapons, they will make demands. We only have tonight. Focus on your desires, choose a life story for yourself—a past and a future—before they register you, write your details in the state register and stamp it. If you want, you can weave a story about your life the way Varso did, and you can pour it into the world's ear like molten lead. If you want, you can suffer to make up for someone else's sins, like those prisoners of war. Do what you want, but make a choice. Choose one of the many faces you have, the one that is closest to your soul, the one that they will end up drawing on a piece of paper and handing back to you. Decide everything now, because once that stamp comes down, nothing can be changed. All you have is this one life and this one night—decide what you are going to say and do."

"Can we pick a different name?"

"You can do anything…"

"What about you?" Sato asked. "Have you decided?"

"I have no desire to choose, nor do I have any options. Everyone knows that I am Harout."

"What would be the right thing to say? If we're asked, do we say that we know you?" Aso was still trying to figure things out.

Harout hesitated for a moment.

"You know me," he said, "We've lived in the same village, we've breathed the same air and drunk the same water… We've said hello to each other every day, and once in a wall we've even asked each other how we were doing."

"What about Haiké? How can Haiké choose a story for himself? He can't!"

[104]

Everyone turned around and looked at Haiké, sitting numb at the foot of a wall.

"We can each pick a story for ourselves, whatever is left in the end is Haiké's" Noyem proposed.

"That's not fair," Vasil complained, "He already has what's left now, is that really his choice?"

"Don't worry about Haiké," Harout said, "Think about yourselves, let God worry about Haiké."

Harout got up and was about to leave. Sato called out.

"I have something to tell you," she said, "I want you to know about the other night. When you saved me, from the mountains... I want you to know what I was doing."

"That's none of my business..." Harout cut her off.

"I want you to know that..." Sato's voice grew hoarse with emotion and she drew a deep breath, "I have to say it..."

"Don't say it," Harout almost shouted, "You needed saving and I saved you. The rest is none of my business. I'm only human, my soul is a man's soul... It can't bear it, do you understand? It can't bear this burden..."

He went home, lay down and went to sleep. He had a dream, the kind of thing you could only see in hell. No other creature of God would be able to tolerate such a thing—only a good hell. He was sitting in the garden. It was like a story—a divine garden. The leafless trees had bloomed, bread as soft as foam, the colors and fragrances blended into one, cooking together to turn into a sacred chrism. The yellow bees hovered above the trees, their hearts and lungs buzzing hoarsely with emotion, and they could not hold back—they would dive face first into the souls of the flowers, sucking and sucking... What sweet honey they must have made! And there he sat. Alone. Among those trees and flowers. Among that chrism and communion, he could hear the sound of the stream. The pure wind plucked from the nostrils of the sky would sometimes blow into the trees' armpits, and the applause of the trees would blend with the sounds emitted by the birds, bees and water. The stream flowed through the garden and under his feet. The cold stream crashes with the sound of falling branches as it carries the water, its wet pieces shattering onto the grass and flowers. The hardened thyme stretched heavily like a pregnant woman, hanging over the stream, the petals of its worm-infested flowers touching the surface of the water.

He sat there. On that warm, kind day. With the sun—the warmest, brightest, most divine sun. It smiled. It provided heat and smiled at the world that it had warmed. The white clouds melted in billows at the lips of the sun. He sat there. The birds were singing with the voices of angels, the voice of God. Their song sprinkled gold dust into the human soul. A girl's giggle could be heard from somewhere, then a man's whispers—the words meant for only one ear… And he sat there. In the middle. Under the sun to end all suns. He was listening to the birdsong. Looking at the insatiable bees, the leafless blooming trees… And the events in the garden flowed like honey, tickling his throat with a sweet scratching…

He sat there, surrounded by dogs. Nobody had ever seen anything like this. The dogs were handsome—shepherd dogs with large faces. They had gone for a swim in the river and were hungry now. And they looked at him. He knew they would eat him. He decided to trick the dogs. He plucked off his arm first and threw it at them. They ate it. Then they looked at him. They were still hungry. He pulled off a leg and threw it at them. They ate it and turned to look at him again. He only had one leg, but the dogs were many. They growled and stared at him. He picked out his ribs and threw it at them. There are too many of them, too many dogs. Why had God created so many dogs? Why had he sent them to him after making so many of them? Didn't He know they would eat him? They could never have their fill. They were shepherd dogs. Clean, freshly bathed. What could he do? He had broken up his body piece by piece, they had eaten it. There was nothing left of him—only he was left and his heart. There was nothing left of him. And there were too many dogs. Shepherd dogs. Looking at him and growling. He curled up around his heart, collapsed on it, trying to protect it so that the dogs would not see it, so that they would think that he was done, there was nothing left of him. But the dogs—shepherd dogs—had strangled so many wolves, they had ripped through so many sheep…

The dogs had smelled the heart. And they were growling. They were glaring at him. Someone somewhere was sharpening a knife, scraping it against a wall. He could tell—that knife was going to pierce his heart. And he sat there. He woke up from the sound of a dog barking. "It's going to give birth…" he thought to himself in his half-slumber, then he turned to his side and fell asleep again. From somewhere in the hazy fog, his mother appeared or, rather, a woman, an intangible creature that had never been, only the thought of her had existed... He was not surprised to see his mother, he simply understood that she was also aware that dreams were a last resort, a final place one could hide. They were both doing the same thing to stay alive.

At dawn, Perch appeared too, at the age when he had not yet lost his mind, back when he would bring him lollipops from the outside world. "Never forget that you have inherited the roads that I have traversed... These paths have seen as many footsteps as the sky has seen souls... A footstep is as light as a soul, otherwise the roads would not be able to bear their weight," he said and vanished.

The dawn flowed out through the throat of the rooster and when it poured out, the air went red at the force of the blow. The first cock-a-doo-dle-doo scratched at the dawn like a stream of water blowing into a strong wind, where it shatters and turns into moisture.

In the morning, hunting dogs, policemen and soldiers came looking for the tinsmith. The dogs ran to the right, they ran to the left, they sniffed, whined, and barked—they had caught the scent they were seeking. The policemen and the soldiers that had come with them could not believe their eyes—how could a village have existed here about which they had knowing nothing? They had even managed to put numbers on all the rocks and the bushes, the conversations that people were having, their thoughts and dreams—how could they have missed a whole village, with its chimneys and smoke, the barking of its dogs, the mooing of its cows, the bleating of its sheep. A structure, where the donkeys would be tied in the yard and skip to the heat of the sun and the beat of their own braying...

The grave had still not given Vardanyan any peace. While the others counted the number of houses and livestock, while they examined the villagers and registered the animals and dogs they owned, he kept asking anyone who would listen,

"What about the grave? Who's in the grave?"

"What grave?"

"The one beneath the village... Who's in there?"

"Oh. That's not really a grave. It's empty," people smiled apologetically, "There's no body there, just the stone."

"What?" the policeman's eyes grew wide, "What have you done with the body?"

[107]

"There wasn't one to start with… That's the grave of Nakhshun's mother… We woke up one morning and saw that a grave-stone had been placed there. She'd had one put there, she just goes there and burns incense once in a while, in memory of her mother. I mean, they were all slaughtered there, you know, there are no bodies left."

"Tell me more about that," the policeman tugged at the arm of the person talking and looked him sternly in the eyes.

"We woke up one morning and some of the women of the village went to collect some thyme—they saw the cross-stone was there, while it hadn't been there the previous day. 'They've brought it during the night. It wasn't enough that we had to accept them into our fold, now we have to take in their deceased as well.' 'If these people have moved here for good, they must bring everything they can with them.' 'They're not going to leave behind what belongs to them, are they?' Everyone was saying something about it."

"During the night…" the policeman mumbled. "But if you haven't seen it, how do you know who placed it? How do you know whether or not there is a body beneath it? Tell the truth…" he glared threateningly.

"Why would I lie to you? Perhaps that day is gone, but God from that day is still here—it's empty, trust me. The Turks devoured the corpse years ago during the massacres… I don't remember well whether it was her or Yero's mother… They'd entered her house and seen that she was baking bread, they stuck her into the tonir and mixed her in with the bread she was baking. She met her end in those hot ashes… The corpse is far away, the grave is empty."

"Perhaps that is what they've told you… But who would know for sure whether or not there is someone there?" Vardanyan had considered all kinds of options so far—a woman, a child, a suicide, an unknown corpse… He had imagined every possibility… but an empty coffin? He did not want to believe it, he could not come to terms with the fact that he had been tormented so long by nothing.

"Are you sure there's nothing there?"

"Unless they've gone all the way back to Turkey and brought back the corpse…"

"Could someone make it from here to Turkey with Harout's oxen?"

"Who did you say brought it?"

"Nakhshun, Harout and his two oxen."

A suspicion was better for Vardanyan than emptiness. You could argue with a suspicion, accept or reject it, spread it around—you could display an attitude toward it, in other words. So he decided to display one against the very people who had imagined that emptiness that had tormented him for so long. "I need to check this... Nakhshun could be a Turk pretending to be an Armenian... and Harout could be a spy."

The red clouds, pregnant with sunlight, stole the sky's stars by the handful. The young cowherder, who had come to replace his sick father, leaned against the stone wall and yawned as he patiently waited until the people would bring their animals over. A few cows had already gathered, barely standing as they grunted into the air. The women stood there, talking to each other, happy that they had sent their animals off to pasture. The eyes of the yawning cowherder suddenly opened wide.

"Oh, dear!" he screamed and, when the women turned at the sound, he pointed to the carriage, the rumbling of which was multiplied by the echoing mountains.

"Oh, my Lord," the women whispered, "We are seeing things we had never seen before."

The carriage came closer and the two policemen sitting inside asked the boy some questions.

The boy stared at the carriage in awe. They repeated their question, got a response from the boy who spoke without looking away from the horse, and when they had left, the boy ran into the village shouting, "Everyone..." as if preparing to give some tragic news.

When the policemen emerged from Nakhshun's house, the whole village had gathered.

"They've asked Nakhshun to go to the provincial capital," the policeman informed the people who stood there, "Nothing terrible about that..."

"What could be more terrible than that?" a child asked, pointing at the carriage.

"What about it?" The policeman was surprised, looking in the same direction.

"Don't you have any oxen? Why use a horse with a carriage in this way?" the child asked, "Okay, so you have no oxen. No donkeys either? Are you *that* poor?"

Some were amazed at the child's boldness, others had not yet recovered from the shock. They could not imagine horses being treated this way. The only one they had—Harout's horse—was used to carry brides during a wedding ceremony, to provide hairs for weaving ropes, and to pass judgment. Only twice had that horse had to carry a load—once, when Sato had gone at night to bring back the bones of the dead, which nobody knew about to this day, and the second time when Harout had taken one of the twins to the outside world to save her from bleeding to death.

"It's younger than Harout's horse, too," Sisak examined the horse sadly, "Oh, how unfair…"

"Oh, come on…" the policeman laughed as he waited for Nakhshun to emerge.

When Nakhshun sat in the carriage, Harout stepped forward to join her. The policeman pushed him aside lightly with an apology.

"Harout *jan*, you don't expect me to stay in this village of yours, do you? This carriage can only seat two."

Harout was upset, but he did not have a bad feeling about what was happening. Although he knew what was going on in the world and the kinds of times that they were living in, he was convinced that time would pass them by because they did not form a part of the outside world, they lived outside of time, in a way.

Sato walked up and stretched herself to reach Nakhshun, almost entering the carriage. She threw a necklace of black amber around Nakhshun's neck.

"Perhaps there is some news of your relatives or your father, Nakhshun *jan*," she said, "That is why you are being called there."

Sato straightened her own necklace and wanted to say something warm, something good and so, for the first time, she revealed her true profession.

"Maro had given this to me when I aborted her daughter…"

Nakhshun looked at her in surprise.

"Of course I did," the old woman smiled mischievously, "I couldn't let someone like her multiply, could I?" And she consoled her. "Don't worry. God is with us."

"Oh, sweet mother," Nakhshun sighed, "It's not like we haven't seen what God is capable of…"

After Nakhshun had arrived in the village, this was the first time a woman was going to leave and go into the outside world. Without knowing why she was being taken, the people began to deck her—they did not want the city dwellers to think that the mountain folk had nothing. The pride that only orphans can feel awoke within them—everyone brought whatever ring or jewelry they had and they poured it on Nakhshun, then sent her off. When Nakhshun was sitting in the carriage and the policemen had pushed Harout back saying that there was no space, the people had not suspected anything. They were still feeling back for the horse, which had been reined to a carriage instead of carrying a bride. And they watched mournfully a long time after they had left and they consoled themselves saying that at least the load the horse had to drag behind them was their very own Nakhshun. One of the children stared and stared, and then asked,

"This wasn't the horse from Varso's story, was it? That wasn't the son of the king…"

"No, my dear," his grandfather calmed him down, "There are so many horses out there in the world… There are places where they can be found in herds, like our sheep… Why would they go after the horse in the story?"

And the people dispersed, each lost in their own thoughts.

After the carriage departed, the men kept themselves busy by castrating Vaghinak's ram—they had wrestled it to the floor and were rolling around with it. One of them held the animal by its hoofs, the other by its curved horns, a third was spinning around with the others, shouting instructions, "Press down on its head… the horns, careful of the horns…", "Good, good, sit down…", "Hit it, hit its legs…"

"He's a strong one! Hold tight!" Vaghinak shouted, scared of the animal's wild kicking. He was juggling the creature's scrota in his palm and waiting for the right moment to tug, "Hold tight… Careful he doesn't stick those horns of his into one of our chests!"

After this warning, the men worked in pairs to hold each of the horns as the ram, lying on the ground, kept kicking, the muscles tensing in the legs they held, his horns digging into the soil, his body shuddering… With this last display of anger, the ram was trying to break free.

Night had already fallen. The moon had gone soft and flowed into the lake and a hollow image of it, as transparent as a snake's shed skin, was tangled in the clouds. Waiting for Nakhshun, the men had lit a fire and waited around it. The dung had already burned out and the flames had died down. The soft, hot embers warmed the potatoes under them like a brooding hen uses its chest to warm her eggs. The people crouched around and dirtied their hands as they peeled the potatoes, then they dirtied their mouths as they ate them. They ate and looked at Harout, and then added some salt to the peeled parts of the potato, ate again and looked at Harout. A couple of them sighed to show they were upset, another poked at the ashes with a finger and took out a potato, which he caringly held out to Harout… Harout chewed it, feeling no taste in his mouth, his eyes staring into the hot, smoking embers; in his thoughts, it was not dung that had burned—it was him that the flames had consumed. The man sat around the warm embers, peeled the potatoes and ate them, they peeled the potatoes and added salt, and ate them… they waited. Dawn broke, the day was halfway through, but Nakhshun had still not appeared. And although it was a dark, cold day—the black clouds had drunk up on the water of fruits and would explode if anyone touched them—Harout prepared his oxen, loaded his cart and went into the outside world. He came back quickly. The villagers could not be held back. They quickly clambered on the cart and removed the rock salt, but there was nobody underneath. Harout took out the soft, boneless fish and threw them on the rocks for the birds to eat. Then he rushed to Nakhshun's house. He did not emerge from there for a long time. Those peeping in through the window saw him going through everything in the house, overturning items, searching every nook and cranny; they could not understand what he was looking for or perhaps rescuing, as he cast item after item out the door. He was upset when he came out of Nakhshun's house, and he did not look anyone in the eye as he went toward her mother's grave, toward the cross-stone that he had brought many years ago, the one that held nobody underneath, the one that Nakhshun had cared for so much that people had forgotten that the grave was hollow. He ran his fingers through the grass as he removed the clay plate from the corner of the stone. He found some dried thorns that were still swaying on their stem, despite the sun's best efforts. He plucked them, paying no heed to how they pricked his fingers, then he crushed them and put in the plate, after which he set them on fire. When the fire died down, he sprinkled some incense on the hot ashes. He waited for the incense to melt completely and then he made up his mind—he would have a second cross-stone place—this one for Nakhshun—and it would say, "For you – the one who never returned…"

That evening, Harout—trembling with emotion and envious of the children who hung their legs near the fire—talked to the people gathered around the *tonir*, "They said that they interrogated Nakhshun and just like that, with all the jewelry still on her, they exiled her. The inspector kept asking her what her relationship was like with the father of the children. Nakhshun had gone red and blue, but she had remained silent. Her stubborn silence had angered the inspector. There was no trial, no court procedure—straight to exile."

"Is the Russian exile like the Turkish one? Do they drive you into the desert?" Sisak broke the silence.

"Almost," Harout replied, "Except that their deserts are frozen."

"Oh dear," Sisak responded, "So there's a huge difference—one is hot, the other's cold…"

After Nakhshun had been taken away, nobody new appeared in the village for another ten or fifteen days. Then the same carriage appeared, the same horse leading it. Inside it sat a policeman that ignored the animal's pride as it slapped its side with a whip and forced it to gallop along the rocky path. Angered by this, the children of the village threw stones at the carriage. A couple of the stones struck the carriage on the back side. The fat policeman, inconvenienced by his own belly, grunted as he turned his neck and looked grumpily at the children that appeared blurry in the cloud of dust. The children ran after the cart and kept saying "Pregnant toad, pregnant toad" to tease the policeman.

"Whelps…" the policeman muttered, unperturbed by that innocent threat.

Harout was unable to calm down after Nakhshun was exiled. His heart was in pain and the only thought that would console him was that everyone is powerless before one's fate. He constantly recalled Nakhshun's bare feet, her transparent skin, and the green veins that shimmered beneath it all buried in the snow of Siberia, and the blood froze in his veins at that thought. A nameless pain throbbed inside him. He kept thinking that Nakhshun had dragged her mother's grave from her previous life to this village, whose grave would she take with her from this life to Siberia? Was he in the list of Nakhshun's dead?

He carried some food with him as he walked towards the river banks to visit the prisoners. It was true that they did not speak each other's language, but they could guess what they wanted to say through facial expressions and gestures. Sometimes, they would gesticulate actively, like a deaf and mute person, to make themselves understood, to state whether they were happy or upset. He wanted to do the prisoners a good deed, as if convinced inside that an invisible force would repay him by taking care of Nakhshun in Siberia. He reached the bottom of the slope, where he could already hear the sound of the water and the voices of the prisoners, and he put down his sack.

The German prisoners—Herbert's left foot, covered in scratches and bleeding, to be exact—had come across the white fox in the summer of 1946, on the very day when Harout was coming back from a good day at the market in Erivan, where he had traded his dried fish for sugar chunks and matches, and at the very moment when he was returning to the village. Herbert was lucky that day, which cannot be said for the fox, and that is how it always is—if one of them is going to get lucky, the other will unavoidably run out of luck. Later, after months had gone by, Harout sold the skin of that fox to a man in the market at Bayazet, who bought it without haggling and placed it on the shoulders of the woman he was with at that very moment, running his hand on the hardened face and cold eyes of the fox while they rested on the woman's breast.

"Sato," Harout had said when he entered the village, "Sato, open the door, I've brought you a gift." And he placed the wrapped carpet on the floor.

Seeing that same prisoner in the distance whom he had first discovered that night, he recalled how Sato had been half-dressed, with wild hair and a surprised look when she had opened the door. She had looked down at the carpet and started to unroll it quickly. When a human hand popped out of it, she stopped immediately, cast a stern look at Harout, and began to unroll it more carefully.

"Could you please bring poor Sato a different gift sometimes?" she had said, "You keep bringing me corpses all the time."

"What can I say? That is your fate," he had joked that night.

At that moment, Sato's disappointed and half-asleep face was a funny sight to see. Recalling that day, Harout reprimanded himself, "What use was that act of kindness of yours, if it was going to lead to your own destruction and that of the village?" He looked once again with surprise at the prisoners that were snatching fish and frogs from one another on the river banks. "I wonder why they keep these men here? What important role could these wretches possibly have to play?" At a slight distance from the prisoners, Onés and the policemen were offering each other tobacco. Harout had only recently discovered Onés' age and wondered why he had thought he was ninety on the very first day they met. And he had continued to think this even after he had washed up in the village, combed his hair and even put on some weight. And he thought the same even now, after Onés had married.

His eyes on the river bank, Harout did not notice the horse and cart raise dust as they rode past him, then stopped. Harout turned around at the sound of the horse's grunt.

"Good morning," the policeman greeted him.

Harout recognized him. It was Arsen, the policeman that had taken Nakhshun away.

"Morning," he responded. "I knew you'd be back," he spoke to the policeman as if they had known each other for years and had just got together to have a drink, "I saw a dream in which you returned."

"No cheaper way to get around than by dream," the fat policeman laughed, "In reality, the ride here kills me every time."

"Why are you here now? Whose life do you want to ruin next?"

"But why are you blaming me? All I did was…"

"Oh yeah, I know, you're innocent. You're an angel, the angel of death for our village," he said and scolded himself mentally—why had he insulted the angel of death like that? What if the Archangel Gabriel would not forgive him that insult? "Great, now I have to find a hiding place from the heavens…"

The policeman moodily got out of the cart and walked to the other side of the road, held his hand under the water spring at the side of the path, cupped the fingers that had gone red with the cold, and drank up before sitting on a nearby rock.

"Things are not looking good for you, my friend," he said in a kind voice to Harout.

"What have I done wrong?"

"What else? You've kept all these people," he swept his arm across to indicate the village, "Prisoner all this time, concealed from the Soviet authorities."

"Oh, really?" Harout asked doubtfully. "And here I was thinking that I saved them. The ruling powers change quickly, after all… If five of our villagers had died for the White Army, ten had died for the Revolutionary Federation, and twenty had gone to the Red Army… there would be nobody left in this village now, brother. But I have protected them, kept them for the real authority."

"What?" the policeman's voice went hoarse with anger. "Do you mean the kingdom of God? Forget about it—remove the name of God from your head, Harout my boy. It will do you no good."

"Sure, I'll remove it…" Harout obeyed, "What could be easier than that?"

The policeman sensed sarcasm in his voice and grew livid at once.

"Your crimes are many in number, Harout, many in number… And you've taken the decision on your own to exile a person. They say the wild dogs ate him."

"Trust me, he was eaten before he even arrived here… A thousand mouths had fed on him before the dogs got their chance."

"You have no pity for him?"

"I know that he was to be pitied. There's no greater misfortune than when your destiny is cut up into pieces and you are forced to leave your life in one place and your grave in another. But…"

"And the biggest crime…" the policeman stood up impatiently so that Harout could feel the full graveness of his wrongdoing, "Was to bring a dead body from an enemy state."

Harout understood what he meant to say.

"I can't be blamed for that," he resisted, "They had all arrived here still carrying the corpses of their memories… Carrying the corpses of their own destinies, they had crawled their way here and were waiting for help. So I helped them."

"Harout," the policeman groaned through gritted teeth, "Oh, poor Harout… You seem like a good man, but… Siberia… No matter how I look at things, it looks like you're going to end up in Siberia."

That night, Onés' cow gave birth—it was two calves, both male, and this bothered Onés. How could he raise two male calves? What would he do with them? One was fine—if it was healthy, they could use it to impregnate the cows in the village but why should he waste fodder on the second one? He couldn't keep it for the meat—the males have a particular smell that nobody would find appetizing. He put on his slippers as he pondered this in his mind, "Harout is as wise as a snake. I'll go and ask him what he thinks."

The door was creaking as the wind swung it on its hinges.

"What's going on here?" Onés walked up to the threshold after going around the house once and examining the closed door of the stable. He looked back—the doghouse was empty, its chain lying useless on the ground like an orphan, the wind still creaking out the same note from the rusty hinges of the door... His heart filled with a thought, but he did not dare enter the house. He called out to the neighbors.

"Harout is gone!"

"That can't be!" Little Harout ran out, barefooted.

"Life is a sad thing, child," Onés sighed, "The things that happen here are always the ones that can't be."

The whole neighborhood got together. They knocked on his door first. They waited. They knocked again. They waited again. Then Onés stuck his head in the doorway.

"Harout?" he tested, "Harout?'

There was no reply. Onés looked with fear at the people around him and, seeing that they too were scared, he ordered, "Let's go," and they all went in.

Everything was in place. The bed was not made, it was clear that he had laid down to sleep. There was nothing on his table—no plates, no note, just a bitten apple...

They checked the rooms at first, then behind the doors, under the wooden tuffet, in the cellar, in the stable and manger. Everything was in place, but Harout was gone. It was as if he had never existed.

"What the... did he ascend to heaven, or something?"

"What do you think he is, a saint?"

"How could he be a saint? What about the wife of what's-his-name in the upper neighborhood..." the speaker wanted to share a secret, "Or the daughter of what's-his-face in the inner district... Those damn Turks!"

"There's a kind of innocence which has nothing to do with being a man or a woman, not even with being human. A saint isn't someone who does not sleep with anyone or does not love anyone. A saint is someone who carries his own burden to the end. When someone dies, they leave their heavy bodies on the ground and carry their light loads to the sky... So, where's his body?"

"They must have taken him!" Onés concluded. "They were threatening him with Siberia, weren't they?"

Snakes were nothing new in this area, of course, but nobody expected something like this from the snakes. Insulting obedience of this kind? And that too, in a situation where you possess both venom and anger. But the German laughed, a roll of raw tobacco between his teeth, one of his eyes closed in the smoke, as he told a joke and stretched the snake from head to tail. He measured a short distance below the head, a small bit above the tail and *snip*, his knife did the job. It's not like there had not been any snakes there before. This was a village in the mountains, there were snakes under the foundation of any of the houses there. There were people who kept a special plate in their yards containing milk for the snakes, or those that played a special flute for the creatures and talked to them, "Dear snake, my lovely sister…" They would bathe in the milk, drink from it, and doze in the music of the flute. In Hamo's yard, they would lie like pieces of rope in the afternoon and the family members would step across and over them while coming and going. There were special places on the bare summits of the mountains where brave women would venture to gather dried droppings from between the snakes' bodies—it was medicinal like their venom, bitter and slimy like bird feet. There had even been an incident in the village's history when a snake had fallen in love with a woman. So the reptiles, in a word, were nothing new. But when the Germans came, the snakes' reputation was damaged. They began to hunt the snakes and eat them. A short while after the prisoners had appeared, Harout had gathered the village people and said, "Everyone, we have to feed the prisoners, otherwise they will end up leaving us without any snakes or frogs. What else do we have? Snakes, frogs, these mountains… I will provide my cow," he pulled his cow forward by a rope around its neck and gave it to Margush. "Milk it and provide curds and cheese for them every day… We should feel sorry for them, they are human beings. If they've been born, they must live." Having taken heart at this message, the children of the village threw down sweet potatoes and *lavash* to the prisoners before running back to the village, afraid of the foreign words they had heard. That had gone on until the hunchback tinsmith had appeared at the village, and the hunting dogs had followed him there.

The German prisoners appeared in the village in 1946—just like that, with their constant coughing and the heaving of their lungs and insides with each wheeze—when Harout had returned to the village from the outside world and found a man with his foot in a fox's mouth.

When the prisoners appeared, the immigrants recalled that the Turks had used German weapons during the massacres, and two of them ended up dying that same night, without wishing to do so. For the rest of them, it was the occasion to learn a new phrase. Everyone would shout the offensive word they often heard policeman Mukuch use—*schnell*. But the villagers did not like the Germans—they were too different. As soon as they caught a slimy snake, the whole village could hear their crazy screaming.

"Well..." said the ones living in the houses near the river bank, "Can you imagine being so happy while you're kept prisoner?"

"Prisoner... prisoner... Is Mukuch really holding them prisoner?" they mocked him, hinting at the fact that the policeman's wife had run away and left him with three children, and he had neither killed the woman nor her lover.

The policeman Mukuch would take them out to the river bank every day and watch over them on the hillslope. The prisoners had nothing to do—in the sun, they would lie down on the slabs of rock, in the rain, they would crawl under those slabs like worms, in the wind, they would hide behind them. In good, sunny weather, they would hunt for snakes and frogs, skin them right there at the river bank, roast and eat them. They would shout and invite Mukuch over for a meal. "Get lost..." Mukuch would mutter to himself, "You worthless pieces of..."

He would call out to Onés and they would sit down next to each other.

"You should be afraid that it'll get worse," Onés would stoke Mukuch's disgust, "Frogs and snakes are nothing... these guys will eat rats too."

"Ugh, I get goosebumps just thinking about it," the policeman rubbed his hands over his arms with revulsion.

"Look," Onés pointed at one of the prisoners that had detached himself from the group as he ate a sandwich he was holding while he clung on to Nushik's wall, secretly and lovingly looking at the geese there. "What do you think he's doing?"

"I don't know..." the policeman shrugged. "They say he's studying the geese, he's a scientist. He takes notes wherever he can—on the clay pots of the immigrants, in the sand, on the walls of houses, even though I've managed to find and give him lots of paper."

"Well, if examining geese makes you a scientist, what does studying the Bible make you?" Onés stuck a finger out and laughed at the strange ways of the world. He chuckled and took out his snuffbox, picked up a pinch, took it to his nose, and then held up the box to Mukuch to offer him some.

That would happen often—they would sit on the slope and chat. Onés would crush that dry tobacco nicely, mix it up with ground black pepper, cardamom and cinnamon, rub it hard, add spices brought from Iran, the names of which he would write in small letters and put into Harout's pocket on the day that man went out into the world, and he would make his blend and store it in little leather pouches that had held his gold in his previous life. He would sniff them—"This one has clove," or "I've added some cardamom to this one."

The policeman would stretch out a hand toward the small leather pouch, stick his index finger and thumb inside, take out a pinch and, without opening it, he would bring it up to his nose and inhale the whole thing. A sweet, spicy, bitter, or strong flavor would burn or tickle his head and palate. He would look up to the sky with watery eyes, gazing directly into the sun for it to tickle him too, to help him, to speed up the process and… "Achooo!" Everything that was inside would mix with his brains and pour out with them onto his handkerchief. The sneezing would continue for two, three, five, and sometimes even ten minutes. "Ahh… thank you, that provides some relief," Mukuch would say gratefully, exhausted and spent after drying the water from his eyes. Once in a while, the policeman would get to his feet simply to keep everyone on their toes, and he would shout down to the prisoners hunting for frogs and eating fish, "*Schnell!*"

Mukuch inhaled the snuff. His nose tickled and he looked at Onés through watery eyes.

"In all these years," he said, "You haven't said a single thing about yourself. Who are you scared of now? Harout's gone… And it's too bad, of course, that he's gone."

Mukuch knew that all their pasts were alike, their life stories ended with the blade of a *yataghan*, but the details were nevertheless interesting. So far, no matter how much he asked and dug around, Onés would simply sigh and say, "God had mercy on me…" Sometimes, he would say "God had mercy on me" with such a sense of glory that the policeman thought perhaps his whole family had been saved and he had managed to bring all his gold along.

"My younger brother's name was Israel. But we polished the sides of that name and turned it into a human one—we called him Isro." Onés made the excuse that his father had had so many children that regular people's names had no longer been enough and they had had to resort to country names. "He was a nice and big child—he loved sweets, while bee stings would make him cry..." They had had family in Armenia and Georgia too, but those people had died in the Syrian desert.

It turned out that only he had survived...

"And at what price..." he said and rubbed the goosebumps on his arms.

When the Turks poured into his house, he had managed to hide.

"I kept seeing the eyes of that Turk." That was the only thing visible from his hiding place.

"He was cross-eyed," he said, "He probably saw two of everything. We must have seemed a larger group to him than we really were... But then the two of them separated from each other—the right eyes roamed along the ceiling, while the left eye went about its work."

"Well..." Onés' sigh was an extended one, seemingly stretching from the ground to the moon, and then past that celestial body. "Do you know how many people my life is supposed to replace? Even if I live for two hundred years, I will not have repaid this debt to God."

"Well, he did have mercy on you."

"Yes, of course He did," he crossed himself, "Praise to the Lord."

"Were you crying in secret?"

"The blood was flowing like a river... who would care for the drops of tears I shed?"

"So what were you doing?" Since he had started talking, the policeman was trying to understand the exact point in time when God had mercy on him.

"I was looking... into the eyes of the Turk."

"How long did you remain hiding there?"

"I don't know—my family was a whole village full of people."

"And throughout that time..."

"I saw the Turk's eyes..."

"You would probably have seen more if you'd shifted in place a little."

"What else did I need to see? I saw the Turk's eyes."

"They killed them all?"

"Based on the look in those eyes, yes. But, praise to the heavenly Lord... He had mercy on me."

"Oh, come on..." Mukuch suddenly got up and shouted, "How can you manage to fool yourself like this? Where do you see mercy?"

Onés got up too and held on to the slab under which they had been sitting.

"Well, what if those eyes had been mine?"

"So his fear has taken on this shape," Mukuch thought, full of pity.

"Yes, well... He had mercy on you."

"The tough part was getting to the mountains," Onés continued. "You're saved once you get there. They'll meet you at the bottom, take you to the caves, give you guns, maybe some food too... I ran to the mountains for a very, very long time."

"It's all right," Mukuch consoled him, "Your suffering bore fruit—you were saved."

"Staying alive and being saved are not the same thing. I didn't get to the mountains, the roads had conspired against me. No matter how much you ran and in which direction, you ended up on the desert. But to save yourself you had to get to the mountains, at least to the foots of the hills..."

"What's the difference? You eventually made it to *our* mountains."

"By the time I got to your mountains I'd already seen so much... It was too late to be saved."

"But, well, God saved you," the policeman looked up at the sky emotionally, "Praise the Lord, indeed," and his words were confirmed by a string of sneezes.

When the policeman's sneezing had finally ended and he took his handkerchief to his pocket, he noticed some movement on the other side of the river. First, the leaves of the trees shook, as if someone had grabbed them by the hair and was dragging them. Then the reeds split up and bent to the left and right, and the policeman strained his eyes to see a path open up with the grass trampled underneath it.

"Harout, Harout..." he laughed, "And here we were imagining you in Siberia!"

"It can't be!" Onés was shocked, got to his feet and stared hard.

"Well, he seems to have not gone very far after all," the policeman laughed.

"Well, he certainly couldn't get to the moon with that aching leg of his," Onés defended him.

Was it Mukuch's fault? Had he been the one to get the news to the villagers and plant that happy doubt into their minds, or had it simply been a coincidence? Two days later, an order was issued for the prisoners to build a bridge. The same horse and cart appeared, this time carrying two different men, who came with a blue folder. They sat down with the prisoners on the river banks' slippery rocks for a long time, spread out the map that the folder had held on their knees and explained all sorts of things to them. That order confirmed the most important thing—as soon as the bridge was completed, the prisoners would return home.

It was the second week of spring, but winter did not plan on retreating. Just like every year, it was trying the spring's patience. Like an animal about to be castrated, it was blowing a cold wind to the eternal white of the mountain peaks one last time, roughly and coarsely, in as manly a way as possible. During the warmer hours of the day, some parts of the ground near the foothills would open up—wet and sticky, like a newborn.

Throughout the winter, the ice would hold tightly to the water and strangle it, stifling it in its palm. When it melted in the spring, the water would explode and splash its cold scream to the face of the sky.

Floods could start from anywhere—the sky, a mountain peak, memories, the heart. A flood was free to choose its source as well as its course… Everyone had born witness to this. The sun melted the mountains and the peaks were exposed within half a day. The eternal ice flowed downward, washed away the half-built bridge, and took several of the prisoners working on it into the lake. When the next one came, they had no idea what was happening. All they heard was the sound and the half-built bridge was no longer there. This time, the prisoners did not suffer. But the final time it happened, the prisoners were blown apart. It had been like a powerful explosion. And it came down at the very moment when the bridge was almost finished; one more step and the two banks would be connected. The policeman Mukuch would tell them that it was Harout's doing, but the villagers would not believe him, "His conscience wouldn't allow it… The prisoners are still eating the food he left them."

"Well, Harout has suffered a lot because of his conscience…" Onés wanted Harout to be alive and nearby, "So he could be the one doing this from the other side of the river."

Who was it? What was it? What was its purpose? The only thing that was clear was that only one prisoner remained alive. The scientist was the only lucky one because he had been with the geese, as usual, he had not been on the bridge when it exploded. But after his friends had been destroyed, he had been forced to leave everything and start building the bridge again, because that was the only condition they needed to fulfil in order to get back home—complete building the bridge.

When the German finished placing the last stone, the villagers stood behind him, waiting for him to complete the work so that they could run to the other shore.

"Stand back, don't hinder his work," the policeman would drive them back from where the prisoner was standing. "Get back… why are you all here? The other side of the river is just like this one… There's nothing new there. Get back, go back home."

But the people did not leave. It wasn't the shore they were interested in, it was Harout. They wanted to see if it was him or if he was rotting in Siberia. Some of them were convinced that the news was true and they were laughing at themselves.

"And here we were, sad that he was dead… wouldn't you know it…"

"So he escaped? From whom? Me?" the policeman smirked, "You don't know me well enough."

"You think he can't escape you if he's managed to escape the Turks?" the wise Onés concluded with satisfaction, "He must have gone up the mountains."

"He's gradually getting closer to God."

"He's found a new river for sure, he must have started a new village," the villagers said dreamily, certain of their wishes.

"Well, let him go," the policeman spat out in anger, "Let's see how far he can go… All the rivers he comes across have three banks."

The process of aging was treating Aso cruelly, very cruelly indeed. His bones creaked, his thoughts would break up, his tongue would tie up in knots, twisting around his own words… Naturally, his eyes were not the same as before either, neither was his hearing like before… In his whole body, only his heart remained young and it would offend him to death when he joked around with women and they responded contemptuously with, "Act your age, old man!" And in order to save himself from being pecked away by chickens and women, he would get up before the crack of dawn and spread out some *lavash* on the colorful shawl his mother had left behind, spread some cottage cheese and herbs in it, wrap it up, put it in a bundle on his back, and off he would go to take the sheep to pasture with the children… The children would watch the sheep and he would watch the children.

"Don't go towards the sunset, oh sun…" Aso would mutter, sitting on a rock and watching the sheep as they ate.

The sky was a red desert—the clouds and storks would slide across, their feet burning. An immature moon had already appeared like a blotch in the sky, but it was not yet dark, and the multicolor lizards would not know the difference yet as they continue to slip by, moving in and out of the cracks in the warm rocks. The small, red bugs would trudge, teeming on the moss. From a low wall that was left in partial ruin—a few rocks lying on top of each other, really—a ball of lizards fell out, dropped to the ground and dispersed among the grass.

"Lucky them," Aso sighed, recalling how agile and quick he was on his feet as a child.

The sun had boiled the air with its spicy aromas of the flowering grass and the hardened thyme; it had turned the air into chrism. An orchestra of crickets creaked the baked air into shards, and the sunset melted into every part of the sky and the soil.

"Grandpa, grandpa, look! What's that? Bears?" one of the shepherds shouted, a plucked daisy in his hand, waiting for the sap to flow out the stem and become a natural chewing gum. He held the flower in the direction of the setting sun, waiting for the sap to dry so that he could pluck another daisy, get the sap from that as well, hold it to the sun… Until he has enough sap gathered that will then puff it, dry, turn brown, after which he could pluck it off—which would hurt the skin on his fingers—and chew it.

The old man strained his eyes, but when he could only see black shadows in the area to which the boy was pointing, he whispered,

"Anything is possible…"

"Don't be afraid," the shepherd boy, who had also strained his eyes and stared in that direction, corrected him, "It's Astgho... She's going somewhere with that German."

They watched peacefully as the couple went down the slope, behind the rocks.

"I hear they've married."

"I mean, that's the least he could do," the young boy laughed, "We beat him up so hard, he turned to mud. But can you imagine? It turns out that he had been in love with Astgho from the day he had come to our little village, and we'd never known. They say he had drunk snake's blood early on, and had gathered strength... Remember how many snakes they would skin every day? Especially back in the beginning, when Harout had not yet given his cow, nor had we given our chickens. Damn them... When we found out, we were so angry with him! Who did he think he was and what did he want with those geese? I loved seeing Khacho that day—he's an idiot, but boy is he strong! One blow and that guy was on the ground, he couldn't get up, he had been flattened."

"The poor guy, why did you have to beat him? It's not like he was her first man, I mean, this is Astgho we're talking about!"

"Grandpa, I can't believe what I'm hearing. What happened to your dignity? Who cares if she's a slut—she's *our* slut, right? Nobody else should have the right to her except us... We beat him up, then we dragged him to the chicken coop by his feet. Remember how he had treated our hens and geese? He had helped them multiply, treated them when they were sick, studied them, hugged and kissed them, God knows what else... Imagine his face when we slaughtered that poultry right there! We did it right in front of him... You know how people take turns to pour a handful of soil into a grave? Well, we did the same—we each took one—chickens, geese, ducks—wrung its neck, and threw it on him as he lay on the ground. What was his name again? Konrad? Yes, Konrad... We were laughing with anger as we called out his name—"Konrad!" But he just lay there in a corner of the chicken coop and we didn't care, we kept throwing those chickens, geese, and ducks at him... The headless birds would writhe, spray their blood and feathers everywhere, run around blindly and smash into things. Their legs had some strength at first, but their knees buckled after a couple of rounds of running and then they fell to the ground and acted like they were rowing a boat... Then their wings ran out of strength and they began to roll about in the stones and dust, some of them even made sounds... Then they shuddered one last time and that was that, they died... Abo got sick at the cloud of blood and feathers. We had to drag him out and we left the German in his chicken coop... You should have seen him shivering, boy was he shivering! Let that be a lesson to him..."

"Oh, Harout, Harout," the old man sighed, "How we needed you! If you and your horsehair rope had been here, do you think they would have risked acting like this? What a waste, you rascal..." he turned to the boy, "All that poultry..." His eyes looked away, bouncing on the rocks, losing the path then finding it again, skipping up and continuing to follow the German and Astgho.

"Well, some of the guys regretted it later, like you're saying now. And when we took Abo home, Grandma Maro said, 'You poor things, why did you have to take such a curse upon yourselves at this young age?' That's why we carried those rocks in his place and built the bridge for him."

"I wonder if the prisoner knows how it happened," Aso asked doubtfully, seeing how delicately the German picked up the girl by the armpits to help her out of the space between the rocks where she seemed stuck. "Who would have told him? How could they have explained it to him?"

"I wonder how those two even talk to each other," the boy said to show that he too understood this thing called love, and he rubbed his upper lip, which had already gone dark but had not yet sprouted any hair.

"Oh, you idiot..." Aso was surprised at the boy's naiveté, "Things like that are spoken without words. And also... sometimes misfortune binds two people closer than love."

Astghik and the German stopped next to a large slab and lay down against that warm rock to catch their breath, then moved on. He was sure of it now—they were going down to Nakhshun's mother's grave. The emaciated German could barely move, he had slung an arm across Astghik's shoulder and it was not clear whether he was embracing or leaning on her.

When they got to the gravestone, Astghik collapsed. She put her head to the cross-stone, then caressed it and probably muttered something.

"She's saying goodbye to her mother," the old man was touched, "Oh, it's such a cruel world..."

"Maybe to Harout too... he was like a father to them," the boy added.

"Oh, Harout, Harout…" the old man groaned, wiping his moist eyes, "You've gone and turned into a legend."

"I mean, if he had to go, he could have at least left Varso's story behind…" the boy shielded his eyes with one hand as he looked.

They had already walked quite a distance from the cross-stone. They walked separately now and at a quicker pace, paying no attention to the sharp rocks, the thorns that stuck out between them and the snakes and scorpions that scurried around. They had to cross a mountain, two hills and the field between them, otherwise the wolves would be out as soon as it was dark.

"Godspeed," the boy whispered, his voice heavy with mischief.

"Let them go… Let them take the weight of their destiny away from our village," Aso said bitterly as he watched them depart with his unseeing eyes. They were already at the foothill, they had been replaced by a black spot.

In the distance, the lake licked the hill's humps and, as it pulled back, it left behind a chilly wind on the moist slabs of rock.

Goodbye, Bird

by Aram Pachyan

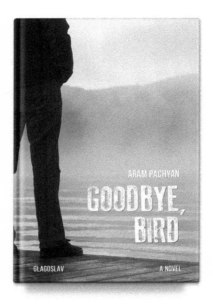

For a twenty-eight-year-old young man who returned from the army several years ago but has yet to reacclimatize to ordinary life, every step, gesture, word, and vision is a revelation, which takes him back to the beginning, to a time when reality had lost its shape, and turned into a new and imperceptible world. In his imagination, he embodies a number of different characters, he feels the presence of his girlfriend again, and remembers friends from his childhood and from the army, who are now gone. This is a book of questions, and the answers to these questions are to be found by the reader. The novel is like a puzzle which needs to be pieced together, and the picture is not complete until the last piece is in place, until the last word of the book has been read.

This book was published with the support of the Ministry of Culture of the Republic of Armenia under the "Armenian Literature in Translation" Program.

Buy it > www.glagoslav.com

The Door was Open

by Karine Khodikyan

The short fiction of Karine Khodikyan can be described as intellectual fiction for women. These short stories with a "mystical touch" tell stories about women – young and old, happy and sad; even when the protagonist is not a woman, the story will immerse you into the life of a woman, revealing her role in anything and everything.

This book was published with the support of the Ministry of Culture of the Republic of Armenia under the "Armenian Literature in Translation" Program.

Buy it > www.glagoslav.com

Jesus' Cat

by Grig

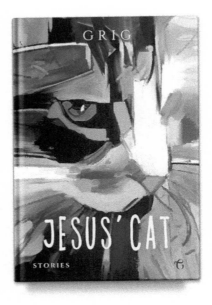

Jesus' Cat is the first book by this young prose writer. The stories involved in this collection reveal, on the one hand, a unique writing style, and on the other, an original perspective on the world and people. This combination allows characters to develop in Grig's creative space that helps readers discover another invisible side of life.

This book was published with the support of the Ministry of Culture of the Republic of Armenia under the "Armenian Literature in Translation" Program.

Buy it > www.glagoslav.com

Girls, be Good

by Bojan Babić

"Girls, be good" is an omnibus novel that consists of twenty short stories connected by a single framing narrative: just after the fall of the Berlin wall, foreign investors feel good about the investment climate in Eastern Europe and decide to open a huge toy factory in ex-Yugoslavia, where they are going to produce a hit range of toys designed for girls: small, plush lemurs called Aya, that will be sold all over the world. Before long, though, their optimism starts to feel out of place - the war in Yugoslavia begins, and the factory, having only produced one edition of the toys, has to shut down production...

Glagoslav Publications Catalogue

- *Wolf Messing* by Tatiana Lungin
- *Good Stalin* by Victor Erofeyev
- *Solar Plexus* by Rustam Ibragimbekov
- *Don't Call me a Victim!* by Dina Yafasova
- *Poetin (Dutch Edition)* by Chris Hutchins and Alexander Korobko
- *A History of Belarus* by Lubov Bazan
- *Children's Fashion of the Russian Empire* by Alexander Vasiliev
- *Empire of Corruption - The Russian National Pastime* by Vladimir Soloviev
- *Heroes of the 90s - People and Money. The Modern History of Russian Capitalism*
- *Fifty Highlights from the Russian Literature (Dutch Edition)* by Maarten Tengbergen
- *Bajesvolk (Dutch Edition)* by Mikhail Khodorkovsky
- *Tsarina Alexandra's Diary (Dutch Edition)*
- *Myths about Russia* by Vladimir Medinskiy
- *Boris Yeltsin - The Decade that Shook the World* by Boris Minaev
- *A Man Of Change - A study of the political life of Boris Yeltsin*
- *Sberbank - The Rebirth of Russia's Financial Giant* by Evgeny Karasyuk
- *To Get Ukraine* by Oleksandr Shyshko
- *Asystole* by Oleg Pavlov
- *Gnedich* by Maria Rybakova
- *Marina Tsvetaeva - The Essential Poetry*
- *Multiple Personalities* by Tatyana Shcherbina
- *The Investigator* by Margarita Khemlin
- *The Exile* by Zinaida Tulub
- *Leo Tolstoy – Flight from paradise* by Pavel Basinsky
- *Moscow in the 1930* by Natalia Gromova
- *Laurus (Dutch edition)* by Evgenij Vodolazkin
- *Prisoner* by Anna Nemzer

- *The Crime of Chernobyl - The Nuclear Goulag* by Wladimir Tchertkoff
- *Alpine Ballad* by Vasil Bykau
- *The Complete Correspondence of Hryhory Skovoroda*
- *The Tale of Aypi* by Ak Welsapar
- *Selected Poems* by Lydia Grigorieva
- *The Fantastic Worlds of Yuri Vynnychuk*
- *The Garden of Divine Songs and Collected Poetry of Hryhory Skovoroda*
- *Adventures in the Slavic Kitchen: A Book of Essays with Recipes*
- *Seven Signs of the Lion* by Michael M. Naydan
- *Forefathers' Eve* by Adam Mickiewicz
- *One-Two* by Igor Eliseev
- *Girls, be Good* by Bojan Babić
- *Time of the Octopus* by Anatoly Kucherena
- *The Grand Harmony* by Bohdan Ihor Antonych
- *The Selected Lyric Poetry Of Maksym Rylsky*
- *The Shining Light* by Galymkair Mutanov
- *The Frontier: 28 Contemporary Ukrainian Poets - An Anthology*
- *Acropolis - The Wawel Plays* by Stanisław Wyspiański
- *Contours of the City* by Attyla Mohylny
- *Conversations Before Silence: The Selected Poetry of Oles Ilchenko*
- *The Secret History of my Sojourn in Russia* by Jaroslav Hašek
- *Mirror Sand - An Anthology of Russian Short Poems in English Translation* (A Bilingual Edition)
- *Maybe We're Leaving* by Jan Balaban
- *Death of the Snake Catcher* by Ak WelsaparRichard Govett
- *A Brown Man in Russia - Perambulations Through A Siberian Winter* by Vijay Menon
- *Hard Times* by Ostap Vyshnia
- *The Flying Dutchman* by Anatoly Kudryavitsky
- *Nikolai Gumilev's Africa* by Nikolai Gumilev
- *Combustions* by Srđan Srdić
- *The Sonnets* by Adam Mickiewicz
- *Dramatic Works* by Zygmunt Krasiński
- *Four Plays* by Juliusz Słowacki

- *Little Zinnobers* by Elena Chizhova
- *A Flame Out at Sea* by Dmitry Novikov
- *We Are Building Capitalism! Moscow in Transition 1992-1997*
- *The Hemingway Game* by Evgeny Grishkovets
- *The Nuremberg Trials* by Alexander Zvyagintsev
- *I Want a Baby and Other Plays* by Sergei Tretyakov
- *Biography of Sergei Prokofiev* by Igor Vishnevetsky
- *Mikhail Bulgakov: The Life and Times* by Marietta Chudakova
- *Jesus' Cat* by Grig
- *Leonardo's Handwriting* by Dina Rubina
- *The Door was Opened* by Karine Khodikyan
- *The Mouseiad and other Mock Epics* by Ignacy Krasicki
- *A Burglar of the Better Sort* by Tytus Czyżewski
- *Biography of Sergei Prokofiev* by Igor Vishnevetsky
- *Duel* by Borys Antonenko-Davydovych

More coming soon...

Lightning Source UK Ltd.
Milton Keynes UK
UKHW012310231219
355897UK00001B/19/P